# THE SWORD OF DEBORAH

## F. TENNYSON JESSE

A "FANY" WITH THE AERIAL TORPEDO DROPPED INTO
THE CAMP

# THE SWORD
# OF DEBORAH

*FIRST-HAND IMPRESSIONS OF THE*
*BRITISH WOMEN'S ARMY IN FRANCE*

BY

## F. TENNYSON JESSE

AUTHOR OF "SECRET BREAD," "THE MILKY WAY," ETC.

NEW YORK
GEORGE H. DORAN COMPANY

# FOREWORD

THIS little book was written at the request of the Ministry of Information in March of 1918; it was only released for publication—in spite of the need for haste in its compiling which had been impressed on me, and with which I had complied —shortly before Christmas. Hence it may seem somewhat after the fair. But it appears to me that people should still be told about the workers of the war and what they did, even now when we are all struggling back into our chiffons—perhaps more now than ever. For we should not forget, and how should we remember if we have never known?

♥

# CONTENTS

# ILLUSTRATIONS

*"Thou art an Amazon, and fightest with the sword of Deborah."*

—1 HENRY VI. i. ii.

# THE
# SWORD OF DEBORAH

## CHAPTER I

### A.B.C.

THIS world of initials . . . in which the members of the British Expeditionary Force live and move—it is a bewildering place for the outsider. Particularly to one who, like the writer, has never been able to think in initials, any more than in dates or figures. The members of the B.E.F.—and that at least is a set of letters that conveys something to all of us—not only live amidst initials, but are themselves embodied initials. To them the string of letters they reel off is no meaningless form, no mere abracadabra to impress the supplicant, but each is a living thing, coloured, definitely patterned, standing for something in flesh and blood, or stone and mortar; something concrete and present to the mind's eye at the mere mention.

Just as, to anyone who does not know New York, it seems as though all the streets must sound exactly alike, being merely numbered, while, to anyone who knows them, the words East Sixty

First, say, are as distinct from East Twenty First, distinct with a whole vivid personality of their own, as Half Moon Street from Threadneedle Street—so, to the initiate in the game, the letters so lightly rattled off to designate this or that official or institution stand for vivid, real, colourable things.

But at first one is reminded forcibly of that scene in "Anna Karenina" where Levin proposes to Kitty for the second time by means of writing in chalk on a table the letters "W, y, t, m, i, c, n, b, d, t, m, n, o, t," and Kitty, with great intelligence, guesses that they mean "When you told me it could never be, did that mean never, or then?" Kitty, if you remember, replies in initials at almost equal length, and Levin displays an intelligence equal to hers. I had always found that scene hard of credence, but I have come to the conclusion that Levin and Kitty would have been invaluable at H.Q.B.R.C.S., A.P.O. 3, B.E.F.

And the fog of initials is symbolic in a double manner; for not only do the initials stand for what they represent to those who know, but in their very lack of meaning for those who do not, they typify with a peculiar aptness the fact that after all we at home in England, particularly we ladies of England who live at home in ease, know very little indeed of even what the letters B.E.F. stand for. We have hazy ideas on the subject. Vaguely we know, for instance, that there are women, lots of women, working out in France, though quite at what, beyond nursing, we don't seem to know. Motor drivers . . . of course, yes, we have heard of them.  There is a vague impression that they are having the time of their lives, probably being quite useful too . . . but of the technique of the thing, so to speak, what do we know?  About as much as we know when we first hear the clouds of initials rattling like shrapnel about our heads if we go over to France.

And if we at home know so little, how can other countries know, who have no inner working knowledge of English temperaments and training to go upon as a rough guide to at least the probable trend of things?  How can we expect them to know?  And yet knowledge of what every section of the working community is doing was never so vital as at the present moment, because never before has so much of the world been working together on the same job—and the biggest job in history.

It is always a good thing to know what other folk are doing, even when they are not your sort, and what they are doing does not affect you, because it teaches proportion and widens vision— how much more important, then, when what they are doing is what you are doing too, or what you may yet come to do?

Gentle reader—and even more especially ungentle reader—if in these pages I occasionally ask you to listen to my own personal confession both of faith and of unfaith—please realise that it is not because I imagine there is any particular interest in my way of seeing things, but simply because it is only so that I can make you see them too. You are looking through my window, that is all, and it is not even a window that I opened for myself, but that had to be opened for me. If you will realise that I went and saw all I did see, not as myself, but as you, it will give you the idea I am wishful to convey to you. Anything I feel is only valuable because my feeling of it may mean your feeling of it too. Therefore, when you read "I" in these pages, don't say "Here's this person talking of herself again . . ." say "Here am I, myself. This person only saw these things so that I should see them."

If you don't it will be nine-tenths my fault and one-tenth your own.

Just as all the apparently endless combinations of initials in France are symbols of living realities to those who understand them, and of their ignorance to those who don't just as the very heading of "A.B.C." which I have given this chapter typifies both those combinations of initials and the fact that you and I are beginning at the very beginning—for no one could have been more blankly ignorant than I when I went over to France—so the letter "I" whenever it occurs in this book is a symbol for You.

# CHAPTER II

## THE FEVER CHART OR WAR

"THE women are splendid . . ." How tired we are of hearing that, so tired that we begin to doubt it, and the least hostile emotion that it evokes is the sense that after all the men are so much more splendid, so far beyond praise, that the less one says of anyone else the better. That sentence is dead, let us hope, fallen into the same limbo as "Business as Usual" and the rest of the early war-gags, but the prejudices it aroused, the feeling of boredom, have not all died with it. Words have at least this in common with men, that the evil that they do lives after them.

Let me admit that when those in authority sent for me to go to France and see what certain sections of the women there were doing, I didn't want to go. I told them rather ungraciously that if they wanted the "sunny-haired-lassies-in-khaki-touch" they had better send somebody else. I am not, and never have been, a feminist or any other sort of an 'ist, never having been able to divide humanity into two different classes labelled "men" and "women." Also, to tell the truth, the idea of

going so far behind the lines did not appeal.
For this there is the excuse that in England one
grows so sick of the people who talk of "going to
the Front" when they mean going to some safe
château as a base for a personally conducted tour,
or—Conscientious objectors are the worst sinners
in this latter class—when they are going to sit
at canteens or paint huts a hundred miles or so
behind the last line of trenches.    The reaction
from this sort of thing is very apt to make one
say: "Oh, France?  There's no more in being
in France behind the lines than in working in England."   A point of view in which I was utterly
and completely wrong.   There is a great deal of
difference, not in any increased danger, but in
quite other ways, as I shall show in the place and
order in which it was gradually made apparent
to me.

Also, no one who has not been at the war knows
the hideous boredom of it . . . a boredom that
the soul dreads like a fatal miasma.  And if I had
felt it in Belgium in those terrible grey first weeks
of her pain, when at least one was in the midst of
war, as it was then, still fluid and mobile, still full
of alarums and excursions, with all the suffering
and death immediately under one's eyes still a new
thing; if I had felt it again, even more strongly,
when I went right up to the very back of the
front in the French war zone for the Croix Rouge,
in those poor little hospitals where the stretchers

are always ready in the wards to hustle the wounded away, and where, in devastated land only lately vacated by the Germans, I sat and ate with peasants who were painfully and sadly beginning to return to their ruined homes and cultivate again a soil that might have been expected to redden the ploughshare, how much the more then might I dread it, caught in the web of Lines of Communication. . . . I feared that boredom.

And there was another reason, both for my disinclination and my lack of interest. We in England grew so tired, in the early days of the war, of the fancy uniforms that burst out upon women. Every other girl one met had an attack of khaki-itis, was spotted as the pard with badges and striped as the zebra. Almost simultaneously with this eruption came, for the other section of the feminine community, reaction from it. We others became rather self-consciously proud of our femininity, of being "fluffy"—in much the same way that anti-suffragists used to be fluffy when they said they preferred to influence a man's vote, and that they thought more was done by charm. . . .

With official recognition of bodies such as the V.A.D.'s and the even more epoch-making official founding of the W.A.A.C.'s, the point of view of the un-uniformed changed. The thing was no longer a game at which women were making silly asses of themselves and pretending to be men; it had become regular, ordered, disciplined and worthy of respect. In short, uniform was no longer fancy dress.

But the feeling of boredom that had been engendered stayed on, as these things do. It is yet to be found, partly because there still are women who have their photographs taken in a new uniform every week, but more because of our ignorance as to what the real workers are doing. And like most ignorant people, I was happy in my ignorance.

Well, I went, and am most thankful for my prejudice, my disinclination, my prevision of boredom. For without all those, what would my conversion be worth? Who, already convinced of religion, is amazed at attaining salvation? It is to the mocker that the miracle is a miracle, and no mere expected sequence of nature, divine or human.

I was often depressed, the wherefore of which you will see, but bored, never. Thrilled, ashamed for oneself that one does so little—admiring, critical, amused, depressed, elated, all this gamut and its gradations were touched, but the string of boredom, never. And the only thing that worries anyone sent on such a quest as mine, and with the inevitable message to deliver at the end of it, is that terrible feeling that no matter how really one feels enthusiasm, how genuine one's conversion; there will always be the murmur of —"Oh, yes. . . . Of course she has to say all that

. . . it's all part of the propaganda. She was sent to do it and she has to do it, whether she really believes in it or not. . . ."

What can one say? I can only tell you, O Superior Person, that no matter what I had been sent to do and told to write I not only wouldn't but couldn't have, unless I meant it. I can only tell you so, I can't make you believe it. But let me also assure you that I too am—or shall I say was?—Superior, that I too have laughed the laugh of sophistication at enthusiasm, that I too know enough to consider vehemence amusing and strenuous effort ill-bred, that doubtless I shall do so again. But there is one thing that seems to me more ill-bred, and that is lack of appreciation of those who are doing better than oneself.

Lest you should misunderstand me when I say that I didn't want to go to France this time, and feared boredom, and felt no particular interest in the work of the women over there, let me add that I was careful to sponge my mind free of all preconceived notions, either for or against, when once it was settled that I should go. I went without enthusiasm, it is true, but at least I went with a mind rigorously swept and garnished, so that there might enter into it visitants of either kind, angelic or otherwise.

For this has always seemed to me in common honesty a necessary part of equipment to anyone going on a special mission, charged with finding

out things as they are—to be free not only of
prejudice against, but predisposition for; and just
as a juryman, when he is empanelled, should try
and sweep his mind bare of everything he has
heard about the case before, so should the Special Missioner—to coin a most horrible phrase—
make his mind at once blank and sensitised, like
a photographic plate, for events to strike as truly
as they may, with as little help or hindrance from
former knowledge as possible.

Human nature being what it is, it is probably
almost impossible for the original attitude to be
completely erased, however conscientious one is,
and that is why I am glad that my former attitude was, if not inimical, at least very unenthusias-
tic, so that I am clear of the charge of seeing
things as I or the authorities might have wished
me to see them.

And, for the first few days, as always when
the mind is plunged headlong into a new world,
though I saw facts, listened to them, was impressed, very impressed, by their outward show,
it still remained outward show, the soul that in-
formed the whole evaded me, and for many days
I saw things that I only understood later in view
of subsequent knowledge, when I could look back
and see more clearly with the mind's eye what I
before had seen with the physical. Yet even
the first evening I saw something which, though

only dimly, showed me a hint of the spirit of the whole.

I was at the Headquarters of the British Red Cross—which is what the letters H.Q.B.R.C.S. stand for—and I was being shown some very peculiar and wonderful charts. They are secret charts, the figures on which, if a man is shown them, he must never disclose, and those figures, when you read them, bring a contraction at once of pity and of pride to the heart. For, on these great charts, that are mapped out into squares and look exactly like temperature charts at a hospital, are drawn curves, like the curves that show the fever of a patient. Up in jagged mountains, down into merciful valleys, goes the line, and at every point there is a number, and that number is the number of the wounded who were brought down from the trenches on such a day. Here, on these charts, is a complete record, in curves, of the rate of the war. Every peak is an offensive, every valley a comparative lull.

Sheet after sheet, all with those carefully-drawn numbered curves zigzagging across them, all showing the very temperature of War. . . .

With this difference—that on these sheets there is no "normal." War is abnormal, and there is not a point of these charts where, when the line touches it, you can say—"It is well."

As I looked at these records I began to get a different vision of that tract of country called

"Lines of Communication" which I had come to see. This, where War's very pulse was noted day by day, was the stronghold of War himself. Here he is nursed, rested, fed with food for the mouths of flesh and blood, and food for the mouths of iron; here, the whole time, night and day, as ceaselessly as in the trenches, the work goes on, the work of strengthening his hands, and so every man and woman working for that end in "L. of C." is fighting on our side most surely. Something of the hugeness and the importance of it began to show itself.

And, as regards that particular portion which I had come out to see, I began to get a glimmering of that also, when it was told me, that of those thousands of wounded I saw marked on the charts, a great proportion was convoyed entirely by women. There are whole districts, such as the Calais district, which includes many towns and stations, where every ambulance running is driven by a woman. Not only the fever rate of War is shown on those charts, but just as to the seeing eye, behind any temperature-chart in a hospital, is the whole construction of the great scheme— doctors, surgeons, nurses, food, drugs, money, devotion, everything that finds its expression, in that simple sheet of paper filled in daily as a matter of routine, so behind these charts of War's tempera- ture kept at H.Q. is the whole of the complex or- ganisation known as the British Red Cross. And outstanding even amongst so much that is splendid are certain bands of girls behind the lines, who, not for a month or two, but year in, year out, during nights and days when they have known no rest, have they, also, had their fingers on the pulse of war.

# CHAPTER III

AT H.Q.B.R.C.S. the D. of T. told me the first things for me to see were the F.A.N.Y.'s and the G.S.V.A.D.'s. That is the sort of sentence that was shot at me on my first day. I have told you what H.Q.B.R.C.S. means; the D. of T. means Director of Transport; the F.A.N.Y. is the First Aid Nursing Yeomanry, and the G.S.V.A.D. is the General Service Voluntary Aid Detachment. Now the V.A.D. I had heard of, and of its members, always called V.A.D.'s, but G.S.V.A.D. was something new to me. Yet the importance of the distinction, I soon learned, was great.

Four sets of initials represented my chief objectives in France, the F.A.N.Y.'s, the V.A.D.'s, the G.S.V.A.D.'s, and the W.A.A.C.'s. Of these the former are known as the Fannies, and the last named as the Waacs, owing to the tendency of the eye to make out of any possible combination of letters a word that appeals to the ear. Of these four bodies, the Fannies and the V.A.D.'s were in existence before the war, being amongst those who listened to the voice of Lord Roberts crying in the wilderness. They are all unpaid, voluntary workers, and they rank officially as officers. Among themselves, of course, they have their own officers, but socially, so to speak, every Fanny and V.A.D. is ranked with the officers of the Army. But with the G.S.V.A.D.'s and the Waacs it is not so. They are paid, and are to replace men; G.S.V.A.D.'s work in motor convoys and at the hospitals, as cooks, dispensers, clerks, etc., and the Waacs work for the combatant service. Except for their officers, who rank with officers of the Army, the members of these two bodies are considered as privates.

And as both the Fannies and the Waacs go in khaki, and both the V.A.D.'s and the G.S.V.A.D.'s in dark blue, it will be seen that confusion is very easy to the uninitiate. That is my only excuse for perpetrating the worst blunder that has probably ever been committed in France. Taken to tea at a Fanny convoy I committed the unspeakable sin of asking whether they were Waacs. . . .

They were very kind to me about it, but when I eventually grasped the system, I saw it was as though I had asked a Brass Hat whether he belonged to the Salvation Army. Yet when I told the sad tale of my *gaffe* to the members of a V.A.D. convoy, they only seemed to think it must have been quite good for the Fannies . . . but somehow it wasn't equally good for them

when I timidly asked whether they were
G.S.V.A.D.'s . . . though they were also very
kind to me about it.

The D. of T. motored me over to the Fannies'
convoy, on a pale day of difficult sunlight.   Is
there anywhere in the world, I wondered, more
depressing—more morbid—landscape, than that
round Calais?   It weighs on the soul as a fog
upon the senses, and it seemed to me that only
people of such a tenacious gaiety as the French
or such an independence from environment as the
British could survive there for long.   I have seen
country far flatter that was yet more wholesome,
and I loathe flat country.   There is something in
the perpetual repetition of form in the country
round Calais, the endless sameness of its differences, that is peculiarly oppressive.   Pearly skies
blotted with paler clouds, endless rows of bare
poplars, like the skeletons of dead flames, yel-
lowish roads unwinding for ever, acres of un-
broken and sickly green, of new-turned earth of
an equally sad brown . . . and over all the trail
of war, whose footprint is desolation.   The occupation even of an army of defence means camp
after camp; tin huts, wooden huts, zinc roofs;
hospitals; barbed wire; mud.   And, amidst all
this, and the sudden reminders of more active
warfare in houses crumpled to a scatter of rubble
by a bomb, there are people working, year in,

year out, undismayed by the sordid litter of
it. . . .

The saving of it all to the newcomer, though
even that must pall on anyone too accustomed, is
that, like Pater's Monna Lisa, upon this part of
France "the ends of the world are come" . . .
(and who shall wonder if in consequence "her eye-
lids are a little weary"?). Inscrutable Chinamen, silent as shadows, flashing their sudden
smiles, even more mysterious than their immo-
bility, turned from their labour to watch the passing of the car; Kaffirs from South Africa, each
with a white man's vote, voluntarily enlisted for
the Empire, swung along; vividly dark Portuguese,
clad in grey, came down to their rest camps; Belgians trotted past with their little tassels bobbing
from their jaunty caps. And, in great droves
along the roads, or, sometimes, more solitary in
the fields, the German prisoners stood at gaze,
their English escort shepherding.

The first time my companion told me we were
coming on German prisoners, I shut my eyes, determined to open them unprejudiced, with a vision
clear of all preconceptions; really, at the bottom
of my heart, expecting that I should find them extraordinarily like anyone else . . . But they were
not. They were all so like each other, that by
the time you had seen several hundreds you were
still wondering confusedly whether they were all
relations . . . even my Western eye detected

more difference between the types of Chinamen I met upon the road than in these Teutons. Of course, the round brimless cap has something to do with it, as has the close hair-crop, but when all is said, how much of a type they are, how amazingly so, as though they had all been bred to one purpose through generations! The outstanding ear, placed very low on the wide neck, the great development of cheekbones and of the jaw on a level with the ears, and then the sudden narrowing at the short chin . . . and the florid bulkiness of them. A detachment of *poilus* swung past in their horizon blue, and what a different type was flashed up against that background of square jowls, what a thin, nervous, wiry type, all animation. . . .

The Germans were so exactly like all the photographs of prisoners one has seen in the daily papers that it was quite satisfying; I remember the same feeling of satisfaction when on first going to New England I saw a frame house and an old man with a goatee beard driving a spider-wheeled buggy, exactly like an illustration out of *Harper's*. . . .

All of which—with the exception of the old man out of *Harper's*—is not as irrelevant as it may appear, in fact, is not irrelevant at all, for it is these things, this landscape, these varied races, this whole atmosphere, which goes to make life's background for everyone quartered hereabouts, and it is the background which, especially to memory in after years, makes so great a part of the whole.

As we went, remember, I still knew nothing about the work I had come out to see or the lives of those employed in it, I could only watch flashing past me the outward setting of those lives, and try, from the remarks of my companion, to build up something else. Yet what I built up from him, as what I had built up from the talk at my hotel the night before, was more the attitude of the men towards the women than the attitude of the women towards their life, though it was none the less interesting for that. And here I may as well record, what I found at the beginning—and I saw no reason to reverse my judgment later on—and that was no trace of sex-jealousy in any department whatsoever. I only met genuine unemotional, level-headed admiration on the part of the men towards the women working amongst them. The D. of T. was no exception, and opined that if the war hadn't done anything else, at least it had killed that irritating masculine "gag" that women couldn't work together. For that, after all, will always be to some minds the surprise of the thing—not that women can work with men, but that they can work together.

"People talk a lot," he said reflectively, "about what's to happen after the war . . . when it's all over and there's nothing left but to go home.

What's going to happen to all these girls, how will they settle down?"

"And how do you think . . . ?"

"I don't think there'll be any trouble whether they marry or not. They will have had their adventure."

I looked at him and thought what a penetrating remark that was. Later, in view of what I came to think and be told, I wondered whether it were true after all; later still came to what seems to me the solution of it, or as much of a solution as that can be which still leaves one with an "I wonder. . . ."

He told me tales of the Fannies who, being now under the Red Cross, came directly under his jurisdiction. He told me of a lonely outpost at the beginning of the war where there was only one surgeon and two Fannies, and how for twenty-four hours they all three worked, "up to the knees in blood," amputating, tying up, bandaging, without rest or relief. How the whole of the work of the convoying of wounded for the enormous Calais district was done entirely by the girls, of how, at this particular Fanny convoy to which we were going, they were raided practically every fine night, and that their camp was in about the "unhealthiest spot," as regarded raids, in the district. How during the last raid nine aerial torpedoes fell around the camp, and exploded, and one fell right in the middle and did not explode,

or there would have been very little Fanny Convoy left . . . but how it made a hole seven feet
deep and weighed a hundred and ten pounds and
stood higher than a stock-size Fanny. And,
crowning touch of jubilation to the Convoy, of how
the French authorities had promised to present it
to them after it was cleaned out and rendered in-
nocuous, to their no small contentment. As well-
earned a trophy as ever decorated a mess-
room. . . .

He talked very like a nice father about to show
off his girls and back them against the world.

# CHAPTER IV

## MY FIRST CONVOY

WE arrived on a great day for the Fannies —the famous Aerial Torpedo had preceded us by a bare hour. There it lay, on the floor of the mess-room, reminding me, with its great steel fins and long rounded nose, of a dead shark. The Commandant showed it us with pride, and every successive Fanny entering was greeted with the two words—"It's come." The D. of T. swore he would have it mounted on a brass and mahogany stand with an engraved plate to tell its history. Two strong Fannies reared it up, for even empty its weight was noteworthy, and it stood on its murderous nose with its wicked fins, the solid steel of one of them bent and crumpled like a sheet of paper, above my head. A great trophy, and a hard-earned one.

This was the first camp I saw, and a very good one as camps go. (I merely add that latter sentence because personally I think any form of community life the most terrible of hardships.) It is rather pathetic to see how, in all the camps in France, the girls have managed to get not only as

34]

individual but as feminine touches as possible. I never saw a woman's office anywhere in France that was not a mass of flowers; and window-boxes, flower-beds, basins of bulbs, are cultivated everywhere. Every office, too, though strictly businesslike, has chintz curtains of lovely colours. You can always tell a woman's office from a man's, which is a good sign, and should hearten the pessimists who cry that this doing of men's work will de-feminise the women.

The Commandant at this Fannies' camp took me into her office, and she and the D. of T.— who chimed in whenever he thought she was not saying enough in praise of his admired Fannies —told me the rough outlines of the history of the body since the beginning of the war. Though now affiliated to the Red Cross, they were an independent body before the war, and when hostilities broke out were a mounted corps, with horse ambulances. They offered themselves to the English authorities, were refused, and came out to the war-zone and worked for the Belgians for fourteen months. They ran a hospital in Calais staffed by themselves for nurses and with Belgian doctors and orderlies. Then, in the beginning of 1916 they offered to drive motor ambulances and thus release Red Cross men drivers, and now they are running, with the exception of two ambulances for Chinese, the whole of the Calais district, and have released many·A.S.C. men as well.

It is a big area, with many outlying camps where there are detached units.' As a rule, there is only one girl to each ambulance, but in very lonely spots the allowance is three girls to two cars. At St. Omer the authorities at first objected to having them, but now they have taken over the whole of the Red Cross and A.S.C. ambulances there.

At this camp that I saw, they have no day or night shifts, as there is not much night work except during a push, when everyone works night and day without more than a couple of hours' sleep snatched with clothes on—indeed, I heard of a convoy where for a fortnight the girls never took off their clothes, but just kept on with frag-- mentary rests.  The other occasion when there is night work is when there is a raid.  As I have said, the camp is in a peculiarly unhealthy spot for bombs, and until just lately the girls had no raid-shelter.  Now one has been dug for them, roofed with concrete and sandbags and earth, which would stand anything short of a direct hit from some such pleasant little missile as is now the pride of the camp.

But at first, even when the raid-shelter was built, there was no telephone extension to it from the office, and therefore the Commandant had to stay in the office with one other to take the telephone calls, then had to cross the open, in full raid, and going to the mouth of the shelter call out the names of the girls whose turn it was to drive the ambulances. She told it me as exemplifying the spirit of the girls, that never once, through all the noise and danger, did a girl falter, always answered to her name and came coolly and unconcernedly up the steps and went across to her car. But it seemed to me that it was as good to sit quietly in a matchboard office and await the messages, to say nothing of taking them across that danger zone. Now an order has gone forth that the ambulances are not to start till the raid is over, as they are too precious to be risked.

It is not a bad record, this continuous service of the Fannies since the outbreak of war, is it?

For remember it is not work that can be taken up and dropped. You sign on for six months at a time, and only have two fortnights of leave in the year. And the girls sign on, again and again; they are nearly all veterans at it. And, comfortable as the camp has been made—all the necessities of life are provided by the War Office and the "frills" by the Red Cross—and in spite of the tiny separate cubicles—greatest blessing of all—decorated to taste by the owner, in spite of everything that can be done to make the girls happy and keep them well—it is still a picnic. And a picnic may be all very well for a week or even a fortnight, but a picnic carried on over the years is not at all the same thing. . . .

Certainly they all seemed very happy, and are all very well. Girls who go out rather delicate soon become strong in the hard open air life, and there has not been a single case of strain from working the heavy ambulances. The girls do all cleaning and oiling of the cars themselves, and all repairs with the exception of the very complicated cases, for which they are allowed to call on the help of two mechanics, but only after the request has gone through those in authority.

The domestic staff, with the exception of one Frenchwoman in the kitchen, is supplied by the girls themselves, and on this subject of domestic staffs in France I shall say more later. Their food is Army rations, which are excellent, as I can testify after straitened England—supplemented by milk and fresh vegetables, while the Red Cross gives the extras of life such as custard, cornflower, etc.

When at tea I saw butter brought forth in a lordly dish and was told to take as much as I liked on hot toast, I felt it was a solemn moment. There seemed a very care-free atmosphere about the Fannies, and at this camp the Commandant was known as "Boss," a respectful familiarity I did not meet anywhere else. Some irreverent soul had even inscribed it on the door of her cubicle. The Fannies "break out," so to speak, all over the place; even the bath-room is not sacred to them. It is a pathetic sight, that bath-room of the Fannies, more pathetic, I thought it, after I had seen the rows of big baths in other camps.

The Fannies have a limited and capricious water supply, and their bath is so small as to remove forcibly the temptation for one person to use it all up. Perched on two stalks of stone stands a long bath in miniature, long enough to sit in with the knees up, but of no known human size. Inscribed above it—(under a fresco in black and white of cats in the moonlight)—are these touching words: "Do not turn on the hot water when the cold is off or the Boiler will Bust."

Everything I have been saying and describing is external, I know, but you see I was still grasping at externals, though underneath certain things were beginning to worry me. But I couldn't bring myself to voice anything I was wondering to these splendid strangers; later, though I never was with any one convoy more than a night, still I got the feeling that seeing so many of them had made me more familiar with the ones I happened to be with at the time, and so I screwed myself up to the point and was richly rewarded. But that, as Mr. Kipling would say, is another story.

We drove away in the windy evening, past the parked rows of great glossy ambulances, and I bore with me chiefly an impression of gaiety, of a set purpose, of a certain schoolgirlish humour and that knack of making the best of everything which community life engenders when it does not do exactly the reverse; of long wooden huts that might have been bare but were decked with pictures, patterned chintzes, bookshelves, cushions; and above all, I took an impression of a certain quality that I can only describe as "stark" in the girls, though that is too bleak a word for what I mean. It is a sort of splendid austerity, that pervades their look and their outlook, that spiritually works itself out in this determined sticking at the job, this avoidance of any emotion that interferes with it, and in their bodies expresses itself in a disregard for appearances that one would never have thought to find in human woman. It leaves you gasping. They come in, windblown, reddened, hot with exertion, after recklessly abandoning their hands to all the harsh treatment of a car—the sacrifice of the hands is no small one, and every girl driving a car makes it—they come in, toss their caps down, brush their hair back from their brow in the one gesture that no woman has ever permitted to herself or liked in a lover —and they don't mind.

It is amazing, that disregard for appearances, but of course it is partly explained by the fact that the natural tendency in young things would be to accentuate anything of that kind once it was discovered . . . and for the rest—I really think they are too intent on what they are doing and care too little about themselves or what anyone may be thinking of them. What a blessed freedom! . . . This at last is what it is to be as free as a man.

# CHAPTER V

## OUTPOSTS

It is a matter of temperament whether community life, with its enforced lack of individualism, or the intense refraction engendered by the fact of two people only living together in a solitude, is the more trying. In the former state one may hope to attain isolation from the very superabundance of personalities all around, but for the latter there is at least this to be said, that if the two feel like leaving each other alone there is no distraction of noise and presences. Either is a test to persons who are sensitive about their right to solitude, a greater one than to those who mix happily with their fellow humans. Both are to be found in their best expression among the English girls in France. From the Fanny convoy to a lonely rest station was a change that set me thinking over the problem, a problem in which I was a mere observer, but which all these girls had solved each in her different way, doubtless, but as far as I could tell, to the nicest hair-fine edge of success.

My first rest station was in an out-of-the-way

little place, bleak and treeless, and consisted of a wooden hut built alongside the railway line. In this hut lived the two V.A.D.'s who ran the show —which means that they do the cooking for themselves and for the trains which they supplied with food, that they dispense medicines for the patients who appear daily at sick parade, and give first aid to accidents, change dressings if any cases on a hospital train need it, feed stretcher-bearers and ambulance drivers, whose hours often prevent them getting back to billets for regular meals, take in nurses who are either arriving or leaving by a night train and would otherwise have nowhere to go, and in their spare time—if you can imagine them having any—grow their own vegetables, and make bandages, pillows, and other supplies for the troops. Just two girls, voluntary unpaid workers, who are nurses, needle-women, doctors, chemists, gardeners and general servants, and whose work can never be done, or, when done, has to begin at once all over again. No recreation except what they find in books and themselves, nowhere to go, and that perpetual silhouette of railway trucks and the hard edge of station roof out of the window, of shabby houses and their own tiny yard at the back, the noise of shunting and train whistling in their ears night and day, and with it all—worst touch of the lot—to have to do their own work for themselves.

To slave for others all day as long as you can

come in and find things ready for you at night—
your hot cocoa in its cup and your hot-water bag
—that great consolation of the women members
of the B.E.F.—in your bed, is endurable. But
to come in and have no cocoa if you don't make
it yourself, no bag if you don't see to it—that is
a different affair, and that is where these two
girls seemed to me to touch a point that of necessity the others I had seen did not. And now that
women are doing men's work it is to be supposed
they have found out the value of meals and no
longer look on an egg with one's tea as the greatest height to which nourishment need rise, and
hence have honourably to set about cooking for
themselves—and there is no woman but will understand the boredom of that—the rations that a
paternal army insists on showering upon them.
Under such circumstances to work is human, but
to eat divine.

As I stepped out of the car at the door, feeling terribly impertinent at this rolling round in
luxury to gaze at the work of my betters, one of
the V.A.D.'s came to the door of the shanty to
greet us. She was a fair creature, with windblown
yellow hair and a smut which kindly accident had
placed exactly like an old-time patch upon the
curve of one flushed cheek. She was wrapped
in a big pinafore of butcher blue, and explained
that she was "cleaning up."

It all looked very clean to me, certainly the

little dispensary, the room into which you first walked, was spotless, everything ranged ready for Sick Parade, glass, white enamel, metal, shining in the shaft of sunlight which came palely in at the open doorway. To the left was the kitchen, stone-floored, fitted with an English stove, to the right the tiny slip of sitting-room from which opened the two still narrower little bedrooms. That was all.

This is the atmosphere in which the two girls live, but, as usual, they have done everything that is possible with it. Brilliant curtains, pictures, rows of books—the rest stations keep up a sort of circulating library, exchanging their books from time to time amongst themselves by way of the ambulance trains, which are thus supplied with a library also—and charming pottery ranged along the shelves. The rest stations rather make a point of their pottery. It is their tradition always to drink out of bowls instead of cups, and their plates have the triumphant Gallic cock, in bravery of prismatic plumage, striding across them.

After I had said good-bye to the golden girl of the inspired smut, I went on to a bigger rest station at a terminus and was in time to lunch there. It was a more sophisticated affair than that which I had left, yet when this rest station was started, at the beginning of the war, its habitation was a railway truck—for the romance of which some of those who were there in that first rush, when you were never off your feet for twenty-four hours at a time, sometimes sigh. . .

Now part of the station buildings has been partitioned off for them, and there is a fairly big dispensary, with a bed for dressings and accident cases, of which quite a number are brought in, a kitchen, a little dining-room where all the furniture is home-made—deep chairs out of barrels and the like—and behind that a big storeroom, crammed from floor to ceiling with stores. The girls do not sleep here, but in billets at the town, but they have to provide meals at any hour and meet all the ambulance trains with food and extra comforts.

We had a very good lunch, of stew and onions and potatoes, big bowls of steaming coffee, and a pudding with raisins, all cooked by one of the V.A.D. domestic staff, who always had to slip into her place last to eat it, and get out of it first to serve the next course. I saw only these two rest stations, each typical in its way, the one of the isolated and the other of the central kind, but they are scattered up and down the line, varying in character according to the needs of the particular place.

At one, for instance, there is a small ward attached, where slight cases, not bad enough to be admitted to the hospital, and yet requiring some attention, can be kept for a day or two, thus possibly avoiding serious illness. Near to this same one is a Labour Battalion, many of the men from which are out-patients whose medical inspection is held at the rest station. Near another is a large convalescent camp, the O.C. of which looks to the V.A.D.'s of the rest station for help in various ways.

At them all there is always the work of feeding the stretcher-bearers and ambulance drivers, who in times of pressure have to spend many hours at their work of unloading the trains without any chance of getting a regular meal. In the early days of the rest stations, when the ambulance trains were often merely improvised, food and dressings had to be provided for all the wounded on board, but now, when the working of the British Red Cross is as near perfection as any human organisation well can be, the men have every care taken of them on the perfectly-fitted trains. Yet there is much attention given to the sick and wounded of every nation who come in on the trains, attention chiefly consisting of the giving of extra comforts—cocoa, lemons, shirts, slippers, cigarettes, cushions—and the re-dressing of wounds, while a great deal as well as feeding them is done for the staffs of the trains, for whom, besides the lending library, an exchange of gramophone records and of laundry has been arranged.

Perhaps the most interesting thing to note about the rest stations is that they are one of the few points of contact beween the members of the

B.E.F. and the French population. Our camps, our hospitals, our motor convoys, are all little Englands in themselves, but every morning to the sick parade of these rest stations come not only the local V.A.D.'s and ambulance drivers, but the French civilian population as well, and in greater and greater numbers. Accidents are brought to a rest station very often in preference to being taken anywhere else, and anxious mothers bring Jean or Marie when a mysterious ailment shows itself in untoward spot or sneeze. The Gallic cock is more than a decoration as he strides across the pottery of the rest stations—he is become a symbol as well.

# CHAPTER VI

WHEN I spoke at H.Q. of the depression I
found in all the landscape around and of its peculiar morbid quality, nearly everyone assured me
that I should find the country round E——,
whither I was going, far more depressing. "There
is nothing but sand dunes and huts, miles of huts,
hospitals and camps and so on. . . ." It did not
sound very delightful.

But to differing vision, differing effects, and
personally, I loved E——; terrible as cities of
huts generally are, here they seemed to me to
have lost much of their terror. I loved the long
rippling lines of dunes, the decoration of hundreds of tall pines that came partly against the
sandy pallor, partly against the vivid steely blue
of the river beyond, I loved the bare woods we
passed all along the road, the trees still not per-
ceptibly misted with buds but giving, with their
myriads of fine massed twigs, an effect of clouded
wine-colour. And was there ever such a coun-
tryside for magpies? Superstition dies before
their numbers, helpless to count them, so far are

H. M. THE QUEEN INSPECTING A "VAD" DOMESTIC STAFF

A V. A. D. MOTOR CONVOY

WAAC GARDENERS AT WORK IN THE CEMETERY

WREATHS FROM MOTHERS OF THE FALLEN

they beyond the range of sorrow, mirth, marriage and birth, at any one glance. Everywhere through those winey woods there went up the fanlike flutter of black-and-white, the only positive notes in all the delicate universe, compact of pearly skies, dim purples of earth, and pale irradiation of the sun.

On the roads there was the usual medley of the races of the world, added to as we neared E—— by Canadian nurses in streaming white veils and uniforms of brilliant blue, and also— for surely the most delightful of created blessings may rank as a race of the world—by the glossy golden war-dogs, who also have their training camp near here, and take their walks abroad, waving their plumy tails and jumping up on their masters, like any leisured dog at home.

But—to my sorrow—I was not sent to look at war-dogs, and so had to pass by and leave the wagging plumes behind. I had several ends in view at E——; I had to see the large Waac camp there, its outflung ramifications, and the work that the Waacs did in the men's camps; and I had to see the V.A.D. Motor Convoy, at which I was to spend a night. Incidentally, I had high hopes of getting permission to go out in an ambulance with the latter, though it is against the most sacred Army Orders for anyone not in uniform to be seen upon an ambulance. Here I may say that the permission was granted by a powerful individual known as the D.D.M.S., though he mentioned that being shot at dawn was the least painful thing that ought to happen to me for doing it.

I was going first to the Waac headquarters, to see the Area Controller, who corresponds to an Area Commandant in the V.A.D.'s and whose rank approximates to that of a Major. She is supreme in her area and only the Chief Controller of the Waacs is above her. Below her are her Unit Administrators, who are in charge of units and approximate to captains, and have their Deputy and Assistant Administrators whom for convenience' sake we can classify as lieutenants and second lieutenants.

This is the place to say frankly that I had heard —as had we all—"the rumors" that were flying round about the Women's Army. They "weren't a success," . . . "it had been found to be unworkable . . ." and, as reason, a more specific charge. Need I say what that specific charge was? What is it that always jumps to the mind of the average materialist? The most innocent thing in the world—in itself—and the cause of most of the scandal since the dawn of civilisation. A Baby.

There is a certain type of mind which always jumps to babies, apparently looking on them as the Churchmen of the Middle Ages looked on women—as the crowning touch of evil in an evil world. If you remember, there was great agitation in certain quarters at the beginning of the war, over "War-Babies." They were going to inundate the country, they were going to be a very serious proposition indeed. The Irish question, Conscription, Conscientious Objectors, were going to be as nothing to the matter of the War-Babies. It is perhaps from some points of view a pity that the War-Babies didn't materialize, but that of course is another question altogether. "Passons oultre," as the great Master of delicate—and indelicate—situations used to say.

The point as regards the Women's Army is that the whole of the agitation against it is a libel, and one which decent people should be ashamed to circulate even as supposititious. Quite apart from the evidence of my own ears and eyes, at various camps I was supplied with the official statistics for the Women's Army from March of 1917 to February of 1918. And of these women who "have not been a success," as the mischievous gossip has had it, how many do you think have proved failures out of six thousand? In the time mentioned fourteen have been sent home for incompetence, without any slur on their characters; twenty-three for lack of discipline, mostly in the early days when the girls did not realise what being in the Army meant and thought if they wanted to go to any particular place there was no reason why they shouldn't; and fifteen who were already *enceinte* before leaving England and which even

the most censorious can hardly lay to the charge
of the B.E.F.     And of all that six thousand what
percentage do you suppose has had to be sent back
for what is euphemistically known, I believe, as
"getting into trouble," since landing in France?
No percentage at all, if I may express myself thus
unmathematically, but exactly five cases.   Five,
out of six thousand.    Compare that with the
morality of any village in England, or anywhere
else in the world, and then say, if you dare to be
so obviously dishonest, that there is any reason
why the Women's Army should be aspersed.

These statistics were given to me at the office
of the Area Controller, and later repeated at the
Women's Army H.Q. by the Controller in Chief,
but on that first sunny morning amongst the pines
and pale golden sand-dunes it was naturally the
human and individual side rather than any of
figures, however startling, that claimed the mind
the most.    For one thing, I had the actual organisation and attributes of the Women's Army
to learn.   I knew nothing.   The actual working
knowledge, apart from impressions and things
learnt only by seeing them, that I gathered during the days I spent at various Waac centres is
as follows:

The Women's Army differs from the F.A.N.Y.
and the V.A.D. in being a paid instead of a voluntary body, in being directly under the Army, not
the Red Cross, and in its members being ranked

as privates. But it also differs from the G.S.V.A.
D., though that too is paid and its members rank
as privates. The G.S.V.A.D. is far more
"mixed"; its members are of all classes and edu-
cations, and are drafted off for work accordingly,
but the bulk of the Waacs are working girls and
do manual labour, such as gardening, cooking,
baking, scrubbing, etc., though there are amongst
them girls of a more specialised education who
are signallers and clerks. The officers, of course,
are women of education who have undergone a
stiff training and been carefully selected for the
posts they fill. For, as will be seen, nearly everything depends upon the Waac officers; they have
certainly a greater power for good or harm than
the officers in the Regular Army, and never were
both the force and danger of personality more
acutely illustrated than in the position of the
Waac leaders.

A Unit Administrator has to know individually
every girl in her camp, though there may be several hundreds. She has to blend with her absolute authority a maternal interest and supervision.
While she has no power to say whom a girl shall
or shall not "walk out" with, she yet makes it her
business to know what choice of men friends the
girl makes and to influence, as far as she can, that
choice towards discretion. She must not nag but
must inculcate by subtle methods a realisation of
what is due to the uniform, a sense of the "idea,"

the "symbol," of it. She does not actually say to a girl that she is not to walk arm in arm with a Tommy or pin her collar with her paste brooch, but she conveys to her that these things are not done in the best uniforms . . . And the girl learns with incredible rapidity. A thing is Not Done— what a potency in those words; in that attitude of mind! It probably influenced the earliest savages in the manner of wearing their cowries.

After all, the whole idea of uniform, of distinguishing one caste from another by bits of different coloured cloth, is based on the instinct for being superior. Was it not John Selden who said something to the effect that our rulers have always tried to make themselves as different from us as possible? Of course they have, and it is exactly the same thing which the wise Pope Gregory VII had in mind when he definitely crystallised the measures for celibacy of the priesthood, and it is exactly the same thing which puts the policeman into a dark blue uniform and a helmet before he can so much as stop a milkcart. A policeman' in plain clothes is a dethroned monarch. Nothing in the nature of controlling others was ever done without dressing up. The marvel is that for so many centuries the principle should have been confined to the masculine sex, when it has such an obvious appeal to the feminine.

This principle when carried a step further and applied to those controlled, by giving them also the sensation of being different from the rest of the world, results in that spirit called *esprit de corps,* which is really *esprit de l'uniforme.* Towards the rest of the world the uniformed are proud of being different, amongst themselves proud of being alike, and the more alike, so to speak, the aliker. It is not a thing to treat scornfully, for it has the whole of symbolism behind it. That which makes a man cheerfully die for a piece of bunting which, prosaically speaking, *is* only a piece of bunting that happens to be dyed red, white, and blue, is part of this same spirit. Dull of soul indeed must he be who can look without a profound emotion on the tattered "colours" of a regiment, and yet it is only the idea, the symbol, that makes these things what they are. . . .

And for most of these girls, remember, it is the first time they have had a symbol held before them. . . . We of the upper classes are brought up with many reverences—for our superiors, our elders, for traditions, but the classes which for want of a better word I must call "lower"—so please do not cavil at me for doing so or attribute false meanings—are for the most part brought up to think themselves as good as anyone else, and their "rights" the chief thing in life; while owing to the unfortunate curriculum of our Board Schools, which does not insist nearly enough on history as the fount of the present and of all that is great and good in the past, they are left without those standards of impersonal enthusiasms and imaginative daring—which should be the rightful inheritance of us all.

These girls are now given an abstract idea to live up to, no mere standard of expediency, but an idea that appeals to the imagination. And how magnificently they are responding those statistics show, but more still does the attitude of all the officers and men who have to do with them. I talked with all ranks on the subject, and never once did I meet with anything but admiration and enthusiasm. The men are touchingly grateful to them and value their work and their companionship. For, very wisely, the girls are encouraged to be friends with the men, are allowed to walk out with them, to give teas and dances for them in the Y.W.C.A. huts, and to go to return parties given by the men in the Y.M.C.A. huts. It is, of course, easy to sneer at the ideal which is held before the men, of treating these girls as they would their sisters, but the fact remains that they very beautifully do so.

Another point to be remembered is, that, far from these girls being exposed to undue temptation, the great majority of them have never been so well looked after as now. They are mostly girls of a class that knows few restrictions, who, with the exception of those previously in domestic service, have always had what they call their "evenings," when they roamed the streets or went to the cinemas with their "boys."

Now every Waac has to be in by eight, can go nowhere without permission, is carefully though unostentatiously shepherded, and is provided with healthy recreation, such as Swedish exercises, Morris dancing, hockey, and the like. In short, she is now looked after and guarded as young girls of the educated classes are normally.

And these are the girls, good, honest, hard-working creatures, who have been maligned in whispers and giggles up and down the country. It is perhaps needless to say that they are naturally very indignant over it, that the parents of many write to them agitatedly to demand if it's all true and to beg them to come back, and that sometimes, when they are home on leave, instead of their uniforms bringing them the respect and honour they deserve and which every man overseas accords to them, they are subjected to insult from people who have nothing better to do than to betray to the world the pitiable condition of their own nasty minds.

# CHAPTER VII

## THE BROWN GRAVES

WHEN first one has dealings with the Waacs
and their officers, one imagines distractedly that
one has fallen among Royalty. , This is
because the word "Ma'am" is always used by a
Waac when speaking to another of superior rank,
till you very nearly find yourself bobbing. Later
this impression is strengthened by the memory for
faces which every Waac officer displays in a manner one has always been taught to consider truly
royal. It is only among themselves than any
titles exist; to the outside world, even the Army
officers, each Waac officer is mere "Mrs." or
"Miss," whichever she may chance to be. The
"putting on of frills" has been avoided with extraordinary dexterity; there is just enough ritual
to make the girls feel they belong to an organised
body, without the enemy being given occasion to
blaspheme by saying that women like playing at
being men. In France, though not in England,
the girls salute their officers, as this helps them to
get at the "idea" of the thing—that feeling of
being part of an ordered whole, which is so valuable.

In the matter of uniforms, someone at the War Office, or wherever these things are thought out, has really had a rather charming series of inspirations. At first the women wore the same badges as denote the ranks of soldiers, but a paternal— or should one not almost say maternal?—Government evidently thought that not feminine enough, and now the badges of varying rank are roses, fleur-de-lys and laurel leaves, a touch which would have delighted old Andrew Marvell.

One of the chief activities of the Waacs is cooking, and when, escorted by the D.D.M.S., whom I have before mentioned, I arrived at the little wooden office amidst the pines, it was to hear a one-sided conversation on the telephone between the Area Controller and various great ones of the earth who were frantically ringing up for cooks. Also a new Officers' Club for senior officers wanting a rest from the firing line is just being opened near E——, and it is to be staffed by Waacs and the cook is to be of the very best. Punch's immortal advice as to the treatment of husbands is not forgotten by the Waac controllers when questions of this kind arise.

After talk of cooks came the seeing of cooks, in a big camp and Small Arms school near. Kitchens are kitchens and mess-rooms mess-rooms everywhere you go, and beyond a general impression of extreme cleanliness, an extraordinarily appealing smell of stew, and the sight of great branches of mimosa set about the long mess tables, there is nothing of particular interest to describe. The point is that all the preparing and the serving of food in this great camp for officers and men is done by women and that all the male creatures are unreservedly jubilant at the change. The C.O. expressed his hope that after the war the W.A.A.C. would continue as a permanent part of the Army, while a sergeant gave it as his opinion that the women managed to introduce so much more variety into the preparation of the food than the men had done. Also, he added that they wasted much less.

In every kitchen there is a forewoman cook— there are these forewomen in every department of the work of the women, and they correspond rather to the "noncoms" among the men. At present they are distinguished by a bronze laurel leaf and always have their own mess-room and sitting-room as distinct from the rest of the girls, but it is rather an influence than an authority which is vested in them, though the advisability of definitely endowing them with more of the latter is being considered. They "answer," as the rest of the Waac machinery does, extremely well.

An interesting point about army kitchens, as they are run nowadays, is that after the amount of fats necessary to the cooking has been put aside, the rest is poured into great tins, graded according to its quality, and sent home for munitions. We are getting things down to the fine edge of no-waste at last, and the women are helping to do it.

At another camp I found the C.O. most anxious for the women to start a Mending Factory—it would be such a help to the men, who, unlike sailors, are not adept at the repairing of their clothes. Also a laundry, he intimated, would be necessary really to round off the scheme satisfactorily. Both these are thoroughly sound suggestions that may yet, let us hope, come to something, though they would be in a sense breaking new ground, as the idea of the Waacs is that they actually replace men. Each cook releases one man, while among the clerks at present the ratio is four women to three men. And there are already six thousand Waacs in France . . . Does not this give the obvious reason why slanders, started by enemy agents, have been busy trying to drive the Women's Army out of France?

Every Waac who goes to France is like the pawn who attains the top of the chessboard and is exchanged for a more valuable piece. She sends a fighting man to his job by taking on the jobs that are really a woman's after all. For is it not woman's earliest job to look after man?

She looks after him to keep him well and strong, she looks after him when he is ill—and now, in France, she looks after the gallant dead, who are lying in the soil for which they fought. Between the pines and the gleaming river with its sandy shoals are the rows of crosses, sparkling, the ash grey wood of them, in the effulgence of the spring light, making hundreds of points of brightness above the earth still brown and bare, that soon, under the gardeners' care, will blossom like the rose. Not a desert even now—for no place where fighters rest is a desert—but a place expectant, full of the promise of beauty to come, an outward beauty which is what it calls for as its right, because it is holy ground. Not only in the merely technical sense as the consecrated earth of quiet English cemeteries, where lie all, both those who lived well and those who lived basely, but holy as a place can only be when it is held by those who all died perfectly . . .

Here and there, among the earth-brown graves, stooping above them, are the earth-brown figures of the gardeners. Every grave is freshly raked, moulded between wooden frames to a flat, high surface where the flowers are to overflow, and above every raised daïs of earth the bleached wood of the cross spreads its arms, throwing a shadow soft and blue like a dove's feather, a shadow that curves over the mound and laps down its edge lightly as a benison. On each cross is the little white metal plate giving the name and regiment of the man who lies beneath and the letters R.I.P. Here and there is an ugly stiff wreath of artificial immortelles beneath a glass frame, the pathetic offering of those who came from England to lay it there.

Sometimes a wreath fresh and green shows that someone who loves the dead man has sent money with a request that flowers shall be bought and put upon his grave on the anniversary of his death. Sometimes, when they come over from England, these poor people break down and turn blindly, as people will for comfort, to the nearest sympathy, to the women gardeners who are showing them the grave they came to see. And a sudden note of that deep undercurrent which at times of stress always turns the members of either sex to their own sex for comfort sends the women mourners to the arms of the women who are working beside them. Sentiment, if you will—but a sentiment that is stirred up from the deep and which would scorn the apologies of the critical.

And what of the girls who work daily on that sacred earth, who see before their eyes, bright in the sun, inexpressibly grey and dauntless in the rain, those serried rows of crosses, all so alike and each standing for a different individuality, a different heartbreak—Do you suppose that they will ever again forget the aspect of those silent witnesses to the splendour and the unselfishness and the utter release from pettiness of the men who lie there? This is what it is to make good citizens, and that is what the members of the Women's Army are doing daily. They are not only doing great things for the men—but they are making of themselves, come what conditions may after the war, efficient, big-minded citizens who will be able to meet with them.

# CHAPTER VIII

## VIGNETTES

THE interesting thing about the various places where Waacs are housed, which I saw, is that no two of them were alike in atmosphere. I had rather dreaded much seeing of camps, but, as a matter of fact, though I saw two, they were totally unlike each other, while the other three places that I saw each had an aspect, a character, unlike the others. One was a convalescent home for Waacs, set amidst pine-trees, a house of deep wide stairs, airy rooms, long cushioned chairs, and flowers, where one might well be content to be just-not-well for a long time; the others were houses where those Waacs lived who were not in camps.

\* \* \* \* \*

Four jaunty châlets, chalk-white in the sun, hung with painted galleries, face the rolling sand-dunes, behind them the sea, a darker blue than any of the shadows of land on such a high-keyed day. They are little pleasure-villas, these châlets, fancy erections for summer visitors, built in the days when this little Plage was·a resort for Pari-

sians playing at rusticity.   Delicious artificial use-
less-looking creations, bearing apparently about
as much relation to a normal house as a boudoir-
cap does to a bowler.   Yet they are charming as
only little French pleasure-villas can be, and to the
receptive mind it is their artificiality that makes
such a delightful note of—well, not decadence,
but dilettantism—in this rolling sandy place,
where only the hand of Nature is to be seen all
around, no town, no village even, impinging on
the curving skylines, the very road up to their
doors but a track in the sand.

In these villas live incongruous Waacs, their
khaki-clad forms swing up the wooden stairs to
the galleries, and lean from the windows, always
open their widest, night and day.  Less incongruous the stout boots and khaki inside, as, though
the chintzes are bright and gay, there is an aspect
of stern utility, combined with an austerity that
somehow suits the blank sandiness of the sur-
roundings.   In each little scrubbed room are two
beds, each—for the Waacs live in true Army fashion—with its dark grey blankets folded up at the
head of the bare mattress; in the sick bay alone
the beds are covered with bright blue counter-
panes.   In the recreation room and the Forewomen's Mess are easy chairs of wicker and
flowers and pictures.   It is all done as charm-
ingly as it can be with a strict eye to suitability;
it is community life, of course, but brought as

nearly as possible to that feeling of individuality which makes a home with a small "h" instead of with the dreaded capital.

*　　*　　*　　*　　*

This other house was as great a contrast to the bare little châlets as it well could be. It also was at a Plage, it too had been built for pleasure, but for pleasure *de luxe*, not of simple bourgeois families. The wide hall with its polished floor, its great carved mantels, its dining-room with gleaming woods and glossy table and sparkling glass, its big lounge with tall windows, where the girls dance and play the piano—all was as different from the bleached scrubbed wood of the châlets as it well could be. Yet the spirit informing the whole was the same, the bedrooms as austere in essence even if they boasted carved marble-topped chests, and even here the Army had found things to improve, such as the making of paths at the back of the house of round tins sunk in the earth, and steps of tin biscuit boxes, ingenious arrangements to save getting your feet wet on a muddy day as you go in and out on the endless errands of domesticity. And, as I sat at lunch in the gleaming dining-room, where the wood fire burned on the wide stone hearth, I heard the girls practising for a musical play they were shortly to produce.

*　　*　　*　　*　　*

A camp is, of course, a camp, but there is a certain satisfaction in seeing how well even a necessary evil can be done.   Where all was excellent, the chief thing that really thrilled me was the bath-rooms.   The Waacs' bath-rooms are the envy and despair of the Army, who rage vainly in small canvas tubs.   The Engineers are by way of spoiling the Waacs whenever possible, and bath-rooms, electric bells, electric light and fancy paths of tin, spring up before them.   There are in every Waac camp rows of bath-rooms containing each its full-length bath, and besides that, each girl has her own private wash-place, in a cubicle for the purpose.   For, as the Chief Controller said to me, "After all, it does not matter the girls having to sleep together in dormitories if each has absolute privacy for washing, that is so much more important."   To which it is quite possible to retort that there are those of us who would not mind bathing in front of the whole world if only we are allowed to sleep by ourselves.   But that is just a different point of view, and as a matter of fact, for the class from which the greater part of the Waacs are drawn, privacy in ablutions ranks as a greater thing than privacy in slumber, so the psychological instinct which planned the camps is justified.

Besides the bath-rooms and the ablution cubicles, there is in every camp one or more drying-rooms, which are always heated, and where the wet clothes of the girls, who of course have to be out in all weathers, are hung to dry. Laundry, kitchens, recreation rooms, mess-rooms, long Nissen huts for sleeping, I went the round of them all, and, while genuinely admiring them, admired still more those who lived in them.

Personally, I don't like a Nissen hut nearly as much as the ordinary straight-walled sort. I know they are wonderfully easy to erect and to move, but when it comes to trying to tack a picture on those curved walls . . . And the girls depend so on their little bits of things, such as pictures and photographs from home. You will always see in every cubicle, above every bed in a long hut, the girl's own private gallery, the *lares and penates* which make of her, in her bed at least, an individual. In a Nissen hut you have to turn your head upside down to get a view of the picture gallery at all, though it has its advantages to the girl herself as she lies in bed and can look at the faces of her parents, absolutely concave, curving over her nose.

As I was leaving this camp I heard sounds of music and the stamping of feet, and going to the Y.W.C.A. hut the Unit Administrator and I looked in. There, to a vigorously pounded piano, an instructress from the Y.M.C.A. was teaching a dozen or so girls Morris dancing. They beamed at us from hot glowing faces, these mighty daughters of the plough, and continued to foot it

as merrily, if as heavily, as any Elizabethan vil-
lagers dancing in their Sunday smocks around a
Maypole.

      *      *      *      *      *

One more camp I saw, on a later day, and
though it was a camp, yet it had that about it
which distinguished it from all others.   For it was
built round about a hoary castle, grey with years
and lichen, from whose walls they say Anne
Boleyn looked down, standing beside her robust
and rufous lover on that honeymoon which was
almost all of happiness she was to know.

Now it is an Army School, and within its grey
walls and towers the officers are billeted and in
its great kitchens the Waacs cook for them and
do all the rest of the domestic work, waiting on
the officers' mess and the sergeants' mess, serving
at the canteen, doing all the cleaning, everything
that there is to be done for a whole army school
of hungry men down on a five-weeks' course, to
say nothing of all the work for themselves in their
camp at the castle's gates, and there are sixty-six
of them, not counting the three officers who are at
every Waac camp—the Unit Administrator, and
the Deputy and Assistant Administrators.   It is
hard work, and endless work, and though every
Waac gets a few hours off every day, and though,
as you have seen, everything is done for their
healthy recreation that can be done, yet the life
is one of work and not of fun, and though the

girls flourish under it, we at home should not forget that fact when we give them their due meed of appreciation.

But, hard as the life is, it seemed to me that at that camp which has the happiness to be at this castle, its duress must be assuaged by the beauty of what is always before the eyes. Buried in woods it is, still bare when I saw them, but with the greenish yellow buds of daffodils already beginning to unfold in great clumps through the purple-brown alleys, and with primroses making drifts of honey-pallor and honey-sweetness beside the slopes of ground ivy, while from beyond the curving ramparts of the castle shows the steely-quiet glimmer of a lake.

For war this castle was built, and war she now sees once again, for the arts of war are taught within her walls. And how Anne Boleyn's roving eyes would have brightened at the sight of so much youth, at the sound of so many spurs! Let us hope her sore spirit can still find pleasure in wandering again over the scenes where she once was happy, and if she has kept enough of innocent wantonness to love a straight man when she sees one, ghost though she be, and if her nose turn up ever so daintily at the clumsily-clad members of her own sex, whose toils she would so little understand . . . why, she is but a ghost, and the modern mind must contrive to forgive her.

\*　　　\*　　　\*　　　\*　　　\*

These slight vignettes have all been of vision; let me add one of a less pictorial nature. The Unit Administrators, as I have said, have to act not only as commanding officers, but very often as mother-confessors as well. Parents write to them about their daughters, would-be suitors write to them for permission to marry their charges, and amongst the letter-bag are often epistles that are not without their unconscious humour. One day a mother writes to point out that she and the rest of the family are changing houses, and so may Flossie please come home for a few days . . . another mentions that Gladys's letters of late have been despondent, and please could she be put to something else that will not depress her? Then Gladys is had up in front of the Unit Administrator, and perhaps turns out to be one of the born whiners found everywhere, perhaps to be merely suffering from a passing fit of what our ancestresses would have called the megrims. If her work is found to be really unfitted to her and it is possible to give her a change, then it is done, but as a rule that is seldom the case, as, rather differently from what we used to hear was the way in the Army, every Waac Controller finds out what the girl is best at and what she likes doing most, and then, as far as possible, arranges her work accordingly.

Perhaps a letter comes from a Tommy in His

Majesty's forces, and begins something like this :—

"DEAR MADAM,

"I beg to ask your permission to marry Miss D. Robinson, at present under your command. . . ."

The Unit Administrator writes back that she will endeavour to arrange leave for the marriage; and perhaps all goes well, or perhaps some such lugubrious letter as this will follow:—

"DEAR MADAM,

"*Re* Miss D. Robinson, at present under your command, take no notice of my former letter, as Miss D. Robinson has broken off the engagement . . ."

Human nature will be inhuman, in camps and out of them, and because Miss D. Robinson is doing a man's work is no reason why she should shed the privileges of her sex.

# CHAPTER IX

## EVENING

GREY rain was falling in straight thin lines upon the landscape, suddenly changed from its splendour of sun-bright sands and blue gleaming river to a blotted greyness. The rain danced over the trampled earth at the V.A.D. Motor Convoy Camp, filling the hollows with wrinkled water and making the great ambulances shine darkly. It was not a pleasant evening, being very cold withal, and snow fell amid the rain, but the Commandant took me out in her car to give me as comprehensive a view of E—— as could be seen in the gathering dusk.

When I say E—— I don't mean the little French fishing village, near which we did not go, but the whole vast town of huts set up by the B.E.F. For E—— is become a town of hospitals. We swung round corners, down long intersecting roads, about and about, and always there were hospitals, long rows of hospitals, each a little town in itself. I was reminded of nothing so much as the great temporary townships in the Canal Zone at Panama. There is just the same

74

look of permanence combined with the feeling of it all being but temporary, while materially there is an air about board and tin buildings which is the same the world over. I almost expected to see a negro slouch along with his tools slung on his back, or to catch sight of the dark film of a mosquito-proof screen over doors and windows.

And the Motor Convoy do all of the ambulance work of the whole big district, which spreads considerably beyond even this great hospital town. There are about one hundred and thirty members in the camp and about eighty of the big Buick ambulances. Unlike the Fanny convoy I had seen, there are at E—— always day and night shifts, a girl being on night duty for one fortnight and on day duty for the next, except in times of stress, when everyone works day and night too.

We came in from our drive in the dark and I was shown to the room I was to have for as much of the night as there would be, considering I was going out on a convoy at one o'clock. It belonged to a V.A.D. at the moment home on leave, but she had left a nice selection of bed-books behind her, for which I was grateful, and there was a little electric reading lamp perched on the shelf above the bed. It was a tiny place, but it was all to myself.

At supper in the mess-room, with Mr. Leps, the Great Dane, lying by the stove and the cat curled between his outflung paws, we were waited on by a very pretty V.A.D. with dark eyes and a deeply moulded face compact of soft curves and pallor. Afterwards, the Commandant, a few of the girls, and I went into her room, which was a trifle larger than the ordinary run, and could be called a sit‑ ting-room at one end, for coffee and cigarettes. There was a concert on, and I was asked whether I would like to go to it, and, at the risk of seeming ungracious, I said if they didn't mind I would rather not. They said that they would rather not, too. I had seen the camp before dinner, had marvelled again how people ever got used to liv‑ ing in match-boxes and having to cross a strip of out-of-doors world to meals, and I was only wanting to sit still, and—if the Fates were kind— listen.

For all the time, as during the preceding days, I had felt the depression growing over me, the terror of this communal life which took all you had and left you—what? What corner of the soul is any refuge when solitude cannot be yours in which to expand it? What vagrant impulse can be cherished when liberty is not yours to indulge it?

These girls, these strong, clear-eyed creatures whom I had seen, day after day, who had at first impressed me only with their youth, their school-girl gaiety, their—*horribile dictu*—their "bright‑ ness"—was it possible that this life should really content them? I am not talking now, remember, of Waacs, girls mostly of the working class, or of those used to the sedentary occupation of clerk-ships, to whom this life is the biggest freedom, the greatest adventure, they have known. I am talk-ing about girls of a class who, in the nature of things, lived their own lives, before the war, did the usual social round, went hither and thither with no man to say them nay—except a father, who doesn't count. Young *femmes du monde,* there is no adequate English for it, sophisticated human beings.

For women, even the apparently merely out-of-door hunting games-playing women, have arrived at a high state of sophistication; and this life they now lead is a community life reduced to its essentials. And a community life, though the building up of it marked the first stages of civilisa-tion, is, to the perfected product of civilisation, anathema. Individuals had to combine to make the world, but now that it is made, all the instincts of the most highly developed in it are towards complete liberty as regards the amount of social intercourse in which he or she wishes to indulge. We have fought through thousands of years for a state of society so civilised that it is safe to with-draw from it and be alone without one's enemy tracking one down and hitting one over the head with an axe.

This right, fought for through the ascending ages, these girls have deliberately forgone, as

every man in the Army has to forgo it also. Were
they aware of this? Or did they, after all, like
it, unthinkingly, without analysis?

I had wondered as I saw my previous convoys
and camps, and I had wondered again as I saw
over this convoy—saw the usual tiny cubicles,
with gay chintz curtains and photographs from
home, and the shelf of books, saw the great bare
mess-rooms, the sitting-room, bright with cushions, cosy with screens and long chairs, saw the
admirable bath-rooms, with big enamelled baths
and an unlimited supply of hot water, saw the
two parks where the great ambulances were
ranged, shadowy and huge in the growing gloom
and thick downpour of rain. Everywhere smiling faces, uplifted voices, quick steps—yet I wondered.

Was it possible this malaise of community life
never weighed on their souls? And, if possible—
was it good that it should be so?

I managed, stumblingly, to convey something of
my thought, of the depression which had been
eating at me—not, as I tried to explain, that I
didn't admire them all, Heaven knew, rather that
I must be, personally, such a weak-kneed, back-
boneless creature to feel I couldn't, for any cause
on earth, have stood it. And I wanted—how I
wanted—to know how it was they did . . .
whether they really and actually could like it
. . . ? "Of course, I know," I ended apolo-

getically, "some people like a community life——"

"They must be in love with it to like community life carried to this extent, then," said one swiftly, and a small, fair creature, with a ribbon bound round her hair, agreed with her. She interested me, that fair girl, because she was one of those people who feel round for the right word until they have found it, however long it takes; impervious to cries of "Go on, get it off your chest," she still sat quietly and wrestled until the word came which exactly expressed the fine edge of her meaning. She knew so well what she wanted to say that she didn't want to say it any differently.

They all talked, each throwing in a sentence to the discussion now and again, but not one of them grumbled. Yet they all showed plainly that·it was not a blind enjoyment—or, indeed, much enjoyment at all—that they found in the life. They were reasoning, critical, analytic, and extraordinarily dispassionate.

I can't put that conversation down for two reasons, the first being that one doesn't print the talk of one's hostesses, and the second that it would be too difficult to catch all those little half-uttered sentences, those little alleys of argument that led to understanding, but led elliptically, as is the way of either sex when it is unencumbered by the necessity of dotting its i's for the comprehension of the other. But out of that hour emerged, shining, several things which we in England ought to realise better, and which lifted for me that cloud of depression which had lowered over me all the days in France.

These are not bouncing school-girls, "good fellows" having the time of their lives, as vaguely those in England consider them, they are, thank goodness, finely-evolved human beings who no more enjoy "brightness" than you or I would. And it was the terrible feeling that everyone was so "bright" which had oppressed me more than anything else. The joy of finding that it wasn't so, that what I had feared I should be forced to take as the unreflecting school-girl humour of overgrown school-girls was only a protective aspect, that behind it the eyes of not only sane but subtle young women looked out with amusement and patience upon a world determined to see in them, first and last, "brightness"!

Perhaps five per cent.—such was the estimate flung out into the talk—of the girls really do enjoy it, the ghastly, prolonged, cold-blooded picnic of it, perhaps five per cent. really are having the "time of their lives," but the rest of them have moments when it hardly seems possible to stick it. Yet they stick it, and stick it in good comradeship, which is the greatest test of the lot. Their salvation lies in the separate rooms—small, cold, but a retreat from the octopus of community life. . . .

AACS IN THE BAKERY

VAAC COOKS PREPARING VEGETABLES

WAAC ENCAMPMENT PROTECTED BY SANDBAGS

That concert which I had felt so apologetic not to attend—what a relief it had been to them that I didn't want to, didn't want to get "local colour" and write of them as being so jolly, so gay! For this again is typical—there are perhaps five girls out of every hundred who enjoy being amused, to whom it is all part of the life which they actually love, but from the greater part goes up the cry, "Work us as hard as you like, but for Heaven's sake don't try and amuse us!"

For, of course, it takes differing temperaments differently. To some community life is little short of a nightmare, but to all there come moments when it is exceedingly maddening. In those moments your own room or a big hot bath are wonderful ways of salvation.

As we talked, from A. came the theory that she was only afraid it would prevent her ever loving motors again; and she had always adored motors as the chief pleasure of life, before they became the chief business. B. could not agree to that. C., who did agree, pointed out that it was on the same principle as never wanting to go back to a place, no matter how beautiful it was, if you had been very unhappy there. Even after your unhappiness was dead and buried it would always spoil that place for you. . . . B. said "Yes" to that, but argued that it would not spoil the beauty of other places for you, which would be the equivalent of this life spoiling all motors for A., after the war.

The flaws in the analogy were not pursued, for D. advanced an interesting theory that the hardest part of it was that you were so afraid of what you might be missing all the time somewhere else. She argued that the difficulty with her had always been to make up her mind to any one course of action, because it shut off all the others, and, like so many of us, she wanted everything. . . .

A. said that shilly-shalliers never got anywhere, but I maintained with D. that it wasn't shilly-shallying, which is another sort of thing altogether, it was the passionate desire to get the most out of life, to discover what was most worth while. "I want to spend ten years in the heart of China more than to do any one thing," I pointed out, "but I sha'n't do it because when I came out I shouldn't be young any more. Therefore the ten years in China will have to go to a man, because it doesn't matter so much to a man." This life in the B.E.F. was D.'s ten years in China, not because—heaven forbid—it is going to last ten actual years, or even that, as far as I could see, it was ageing her at all, but simply because while she was doing it she couldn't be doing anything else. She had had to burn her boats.

Now that, to a certain temperament, means a great deal, and it is one of the things, if not the chief thing, that marks service in France off from

equally hard work at home, and makes it, for reasons outside the work, so much harder.

All natures are not the same as D.'s, of course.
To one girl a certain thing is the hardship, to another a different thing. But the point is that the
hardship is there, not physical, but mental, and to
me it was the most exquisite discovery I could
have made in the whole of France. For the finer
the instrument, the more fine it is of it to per-
form the work, and the more finely will that work,
in the long run, be done.

# CHAPTER X

## NIGHT

Not being among the lucky creatures who can fall happily to sleep when they know they are to be called at one o'clock, I lay in my tiny bed and revelled in that wonderful story of "The Bridge Builders" out of "The Day's Work," till the sound of the storm without became the voice of Mother Gunga. Then I turned out the light and lay and listened to the truly fiendish train whistles which no reading could have transmuted, and wondered why it is that French engine drivers apparently pay no attention to signals, but just go on whistling till they are answered, like someone who goes on ringing a bell till at length the door is opened. The rain was turning to snow, so there was less of that steady tinkling from without with which running water fills the world. I lay and listened; and the whistles and the bellying of the chintz curtain and the occasional swish of a heavy gust against the side of the hut were at last beginning to blend in one blur in my mind when a girl came softly into my room and whispered that it was time to dress.

That utter quietness of the girls was a thing that had impressed me after staying in hotels full of the British Army, which goes to bed at midnight, bangs its doors, throws its boots outside, shouts from room to room, and begins the whole process, reversed, at about six o'clock the next morning. Here the girls wore soundless slippers, so that those who had to be about should not disturb those who slept, and doors were opened and shut with a cotton-wool care which appealed to me, or would have, if I hadn't had to get up.

When I was dressed I found my way down endless blowy corridors, for the doors at the ends are always kept open, to the room of the girl who had called me. She looked at my fur coat and said it would get spoilt. I replied with great truth that it was past spoiling, but she took it off me, whipped my cap from my head, and the girls proceeded to dress me. They pulled a leather cap with ear-pieces down on my head and stuffed me into woolly jackets and wound my neck up in a comforter and finished up with a huge leather coat and a pair of fur gloves like bear's paws, so that when all was done I couldn't bend and had to be hoisted quite stiff up to the front of the ambulance.

But first we all went into the kitchen, where part of the domestic staff sits up all night to prepare food for the night drivers. There we drank the loveliest cocoa I ever met, the sort the spoon would stand up in, piping hot, out of huge bowls. Then my driver and the section leader for the night led me across the soaking park to where, in almost total darkness, girls were busy with their ambulances. I was hoisted up beside my driver and endeavoured clumsily with my bear's paws to fasten the canvas flap back across the side as I was bidden. I may say that I felt extraordinarily clumsy amongst these girls, most of whom could have put me in their pockets. They knew so exactly what to do, their movements were all so perfectly adjusted to their needs, they knew where everything was, while I fumbled for steps and hoped for the best. . . . They made me feel, in the beautiful way they shepherded me, that I was a silly useless female and that they were grave chivalrous young men; they watched over me with just that matter-of-fact care.

To me it was all wonderful, that experience. To the girls, who do it every night, every alternate fortnight, year in, year out, the thrill of it has naturally gone long since; the wonder is that to them all remains the pity of it. We swung out of the park into the road. There was no moon, the stars were mostly hidden by the heavy clouds, the sleet blew in gusts against the wind screen. We went at a good pace, bound for a Canadian hospital, and then for a station beyond E——, where the train was waiting, for this was what is called an "evacuation" that I was going to see.

No train of wounded was due in that night, and the Convoy's business was to take men who were being sent elsewhere from the hospitals to the train.

We stopped in front of a shadow hospital, set in a town of shadow-huts, and a door opened to show an oblong of orange light, and send a paler shaft widening out into the night towards the sleek side of our ambulance.

We heard the men being placed in the ambulance, the word was given, and again we set off through the night, this time so slowly, so carefully, for we carried that which must not be jarred one hair's breadth more than could be helped. We crept along the roads, past the pines that showed as patches of denser blackness against the sky, past the sand-dunes that glimmered ghostly, past the blots of shadow made by every shrub and tree-trunk, and behind and before us crawled other ambulances, laden even as we.

The station was wrapped in darkness, save for a hanging light here and there, and an occasional uncurtained window in the waiting train. We drew up under a light, where a sergeant was waiting.

"Four from No. 7 Canadian," said my driver crisply. The sergeant repeated, looked at a list he carried and marked our cases off it duly, then told us the number of the compartment where we should stop. The ambulance slid on, very slowly, beside the train and slowly came to rest.

I could see into the white-painted interior of the train, could see the shelves running along its sides, and on the shelves, making oblong shapes of darkness against all the white, men laid straightly . . . in front of us the Red Cross orderlies were sliding men down on stretchers from the shelves of an ambulance, slipping them out, carrying them up into the train and packing them on the shelves like fragile and precious parcels.

And suddenly it seemed to me there was something profoundly touching about the sight of a man lying flat and helpless, shoved here and there, in spite of all the care and kindness with which it was accomplished. It is a thing wrong in essence, it seems an outrage on Nature—I got an odd feeling that there was something wrong and unnatural about the mere posture of lying-down that I never thought of before. The world seemed suddenly to have become deformed, as a monster is deformed who is born distorted. It shouldn't be possible to slide men on to shelves like this. . . .

The girl at the wheel pushed back the little shutter set in the front of the ambulance and we looked into the dimly-lit interior. I could see the crowns of four heads, the jut of brow beyond them, the upward peak of the feet under the grey blankets, pale hands, one pair thin as a child's, that lay limply along the edge of the stretchers.

The orderlies came to the open door, one man
mounted within, and the top stretcher from one
side was slipped along its grooves and dis-
appeared, tilted into the night. The boy on the
top stretcher the other side turned his head lan-
guidly and watched—I could see a pale cheek,
foreshortened from where I sat, a sweep of long
dark eyelashes, the curve of the drooping upper
lip. His turn came, and, passive, he too was slid
out, then the two men below were carried away
and up into the train. The ambulance was empty.

We turned in a circle over the muddy yard and
started off again, stopping again by the sergeant
to get our orders.

"Number 4," said the sergeant, and we swung,
once more at a good pace, along the heavy roads,
took fresh turnings about and about in the city
of hospital huts, and drew up at Number 4.

Again we were loaded, and again we crept back
along the roads where we had a few minutes before gone so swiftly, meeting empty cars, keeping
in line behind those laden like ourselves. Again
we slowed down by the waiting sergeant to say,
"Two stretchers and two sitters from Four."
He echoed us, and we crept on to the appointed
carriage and stopped. So it went on through
a couple of hours, ambulance after ambulance
swiftly leaving the station, slowly coming back,
all drawing up gently by the train, each, opened,
making a faint square of light in the velvet dark-

ness. ¦And then, at last, when it was all over, the
return, swift again, towards the camp.

We bumped along the road, the dim pines falling away into the shadows behind, a very mild
funnel of light showing us a scrap of the way
before us and of hedge on either side, the twigs
of it perpetually springing out palely to die away
once more.    The wind was behind us and the
screen clear; far ahead of us on the road was an
empty ambulance with its curtains drawn back,
bare but for its empty stretchers and dark blankets, which made, in the pale glow of the white-
painted interior, a sinister Face—two hollow eyes
and a wide mouth—that fled through the night,
always keeping the same distance ahead, grimac-
ing at me, like an image of the Death's Head of
War. . . . I was glad when it swung round a
turning and was lost to us.

We drove into the unrelieved darkness of the
convoy park and drew up with precision in our
place, I wrestled again with the flap, and we got
out into the wet sleet, half-snow, half-rain.    My
driver covered up the bonnet with tarpaulin,
turned off the lights, and we went across to the
kitchen.    It was half-past three, and we were the
first to come back; we asked for bowls of soup
and stood sipping them and munching sandwiches
that lay ready cut in piles upon the table.

Then, one ofter another, the drivers entered
. . . pulling off their great gloves as they came,

stamping the snow from their boots. They stood about, drinking from their steaming bowls, bright-eyed, apparently untired, throwing little quick scraps of talk to each other—about the slowness of "St. John's" on this particular night, who hadn't their cases ready and kept one or two ambulances "simply ages"; or the engine trouble developed by one car which still kept it out somewhere on the road. And I stood and listened and watched them, and I received an impression of extraordinary beauty.

These girls, with their leather caps coming down to their brows and over their ears, looked like splendid young airmen, their clear, bold faces coming out from between the leather flaps. They were not pretty, they were touched with something finer, some quality of radiance only increased by their utter unconsciousness of it. Each girl, with her clear face, her round, close head, her stamping feet and strong, cold hands, seemed so intensely alive within the dark globe of the night, that her life was heightened to a point not earthly, as though she were a visitant from the snows or fields I had not seen, fields Olympian. . . . And as each came swinging in—"*vera incessu patuit dea. , . .*"

I could have wished them there for ever, like some sculptured frieze, so lovely was the rightness and the inspiration of it.

But I went to my bed, and one of the goddesses

insisted on refilling my hot-water bag, though assured her it would be quite well as it was, and was unwound from my swaddling clothes and left to dream.

# CHAPTER XI

## "AND THE BRIGHT EYES OF DANGER"

SINCE the beginning of things women have been mixed up in war, and it is only as the world has become more civilised (if in view of the present one can make that assertion) that their place in it has been questioned. The whole question of the civilian population has taken on a different aspect since the outbreak of this war, owing to the extraordinary and unprecedented penalties attached to the civilian status by Germany, but the sub-division labelled "Women" has perhaps undergone more revision than any. It has undergone so much revision, in fact, that women have, in large masses, ceased to be civilians and are ranked as the Army.

If it be frankly conceded that it is as natural for women to want to get to the war as men, one clears the way for profitable discussion without wasting time while the outworn epithets of "unwomanly" and "sensation-hunters" are flung through the air to the great obscuring thereof. The delight in danger for its own sake is common to all human beings, to the young as an intoxi-

cant, to the old as a drug. It is not the least
of the tragedies of woman that this is a delight
in which she is so seldom able to indulge.

When the war broke, everyone wanted to go and
see what it was like, and it is merely useless to
observe that this was treating it as a huge picnic.
Before the tightening-up process began, in the
wonderful days when the war was still fluid, it
was possible to get out to the front—the real
front—on all sorts of excuses. The tightening-up
was necessary, and all too slow, but let us not,
because of that, fall into the error of calling the
instinct which urged non-combatants "mere" curi-
osity, as though that were not the greatest of the
gifts of the gods, without which nothing is done.

Among these non-combatants who wanted to
see the war were many women, and if, mixed with
their patriotism and desire to help, went a streak
of that love of danger which is no disgrace to a
man—why, I maintain that it is no disgrace to a
woman either, but as natural an instinct as that
which drives one to a wayside orchard if one is
hungry.

There is nothing sooner slaked, for the time
being, than this inherent love of danger. Men
who wanted the fun of it at the beginning of the
war are heartily sick of it now, though they
wouldn't be out of it for worlds. But most of the
women haven't been allowed enough danger to get
sick of it, and so, in patches of young women you

meet working in France, the old craving still lifts
its head. I came across a delightful streak of it
at T——, the oldest big convoy in France.

The garage, over which the girls live, for their
camp is still a-building, is set in the eye of the
cold winter winds on the top of a hill overlooking
the sea. It was snowing heavily as I drove up,
great fat flakes of snow that wove and interwove
in the air in the way that only snowflakes can, so
that sometimes they look as though they were
falling upwards. The long line of the wooden
garage showed dark in the background, in the
space before it the ambulances stood about, but
the girls were fox-trotting in couples all about
them, their big rubber boots shuffling up little
clouds of snow; on the head of one girl was
swathed a greenish-blue handkerchief, which
made a lovely note of colour against the swirling
whiteness.

I was taken in through the garage, where two
drivers were painting their cars—for all painting
is done by the girls, sometimes with unexpected
effects, as on one car which I saw, where "Eve"
from the *Tatler* and her little dog were depicted
in front of the body—and up a flight of wooden
stairs with an out-of-doors landing on top, to
the cubicles, which opened off on either side of
the open-ended passage for the whole length of
the building. Here, in one of the little bedrooms
for two, we had a meal of cocoa and cake, known

as the "elevener," for the obvious reason that it is consumed at eleven every morning. It was all quite different from my evening at the convoy at E——, but equally stimulating.

The great plaint of the girls was that they weren't allowed nearer the fighting line, and I heard a story of how, in the early days, two cars had managed to get right through to Poperinghe, when that town was the centre of the Boche's attentions, by the simple expedient of the girl-drivers turning up their coat collars, pulling their peaked caps well down over their eyes, and just going ahead. They had a lovely time in Poperinghe and lunched under shell-fire, and when the military, including the Staff, were sitting in cellars, the "Chaufferettes" sallied forth and bought picture post-cards.

"It's a shame they won't let us go up to the line now——"

"Yes, indeed," put in another very seriously, as though she were adding the last uncontrovertible proof to the perfidy of the authorities—"They let the sisters get shelled, so why shouldn't they let us?"

Isn't that a delightful spirit, and, I beg leave to insist, a perfectly natural and proper one? Any decent human being would like to be shelled—who hasn't been shelled too much. It is like being in love—a thing that ought to happen at least once to everybody.

One of my hostesses was a violinist and plays at all the concerts for the wounded which take place thereabouts. I asked her whether she didn't find the work ruination to her fingers for the violin, but all she said carelessly was that they had been ruined for three years now, but it didn't matter, as anyway she couldn't have practised even if she had the time, since there were always some girls trying to sleep.

And what do the local French people think of these young girls in their midst, who work like men and are out in all weathers and drive the soldiers wounded in the great common cause? They are quite charming to them, and indeed, when they first came, the French met them at every station with bouquets of flowers, so that the girls, pleased and embarrassed, English fashion, had a triumphal progress. But there are some of the French neighbours who think the life must be very hard on the poor things, and when, a little while ago, the Convoy organised a paper chase, the popular belief was that the hares were escaping from the rigours of life. . . . When the panting hares asked wayfaring traps for a lift, it was refused them, as, though the kindly drivers had every sympathy with the projected escape, they were not going to assist them to defy authority!

The hardships which this Convoy had undergone I did not hear about from them, but from their Commandant. She told me of three weeks

at the beginning of things, when there were no
fires, no hot water, except a little always simmer-
ing for pouring into the radiators of the cars
when there came a night call—for the snow was
frozen on the ground all those three weeks and
the water in the jugs was ice.  The girls didn't
talk about that because they were not interested
in it, but neither would they talk about one other
thing, though for a very different reason—and
that was of the time when, after the great German gas attacks at Nieuport, they had to drive
the gassed men who came on the hospital trains.
. . . You can't get them now to describe what
that was like, nor would you have tried, warned
by the sudden change of voice in which they even
mentioned it.

There was one point in which this Convoy
seemed to me to touch the extreme of abnegation
attained by the G.S.V.A.D.'s.  I had seen much
earlier in my visit a G.S.V.A.D. Convoy, but have
not mentioned it because I saw it before I had
really grasped essentials, and it appeared to me
then just a plain Convoy, and as the bare facts
of it were not as spectacular as those relating to
the Fannies, I chose the latter to write about.

The G.S.V.A.D.'s, as I have said, rank as privates, and among them are workers of every kind
—scrubbers, cooks, dispensers, clerks, motor drivers.  This G.S.V.A.D. convoy which I had seen
was made up of girls who had exchanged from

V.A.D. convoys, mostly from this very one at
T—— where I now was; and so they happened
to be all friends and all girls of gentle birth. But
when I saw their quarters—in a couple of tall
French houses that had been converted to the
purpose—I was very upset by the terrible fact that
the girls had to share bedrooms. In all the camps
I had seen since, both of Fannies and V.A.D.'s,
each girl had her own tiny room which she cherished as her own soul—which, indeed, is what it
amounts to. And the Waac officers, of course,
have their own private rooms, though the girls
sleep in dormitories. This convoy at T—— was
the only voluntary one I had come across where
the inestimable privilege of solitude was missing,
though that will be put right when the new camp
is built.

And here I may mention that, deeply as I admire all the girls who are working so splendidly
in France, I think perhaps my meed of admiration
brims highest for those members of the G.S.V.A.
D.'s who are gently born, for this very reason
of the sleeping accommodation. Let us be frank,
and admit that for the generality of working girls,
such as the Waacs and a large proportion of the
G.S.V.A.D.'s, it is not nearly so great a hardship
to sleep in dormitories as it is for girls who
have, as a matter of course, always been accustomed to privacy. It is not so bad in the case
of members of a G.S. convoy such as that I have

mentioned, where the girls are all friends, but what of those ladies who live in the big camps and sleep in long huts with other girls of every class, all, doubtless, decent good girls, but, in the nature of things, often girls with whom any ground of meeting must be limited to the barest commonalties of life? Also sometimes those in authority—those who are and always were professionals, not amateurs—have been known to use the power given to them, by the inferior rating of these girls, to make them rather miserable.

Personally, I have long had a theory, which will doubtless bring down on me howls of rage from those who will say I am decrying the most noble of professions, that women are not meant to be nurses. It brings out all that is worst in them. The love of routine for its own sake, that deadly snare to which women and Government officials succumb so much more easily than do men, is fostered in them. And so is the love of authority for their own sakes, which is almost worse. It has taken nothing less than this way to show what splendid creatures nurses are under their starched aprons. In times of peace only amateur women should be nurses; for it may be observed that the V.A.D. nurses, though they have had long enough to do it in, have not developed the subtle disease of nursitis. Evidently nursing is a thing, like love-making, which should never become a profession.

I was glad to have seen all the different convoys I had, because no two had been to me alike, and to each I am indebted for a differing expression of the same vision, which is the vision splendid of a duty undertaken gladly and sustained with courage. From my first convoys—the Fannies and the G.S.V.A.D.'s—I got the wonderful facts of it, at the V.A.D. Convoy at E—— I caught that side of it which I was most glad of all to encounter, and at the V.A.D. Convoy at T—— I found that delightful spirit of sheer joy in danger which is too precious to be allowed to die out of the world just because there happens to be, at present, such a great deal too much danger let loose upon it.

# CHAPTER XII

## REST

THE snow danced in a fine white mist over the ploughed fields, and drove perpetually against the northerly sides of the tall bare tree-trunks that lined the way for miles, hardly finding a hold upon the smooth flanks of the planes, but sinking into the rough-barked limes till they looked dappled with their brown ridges and the white veining, and oddly as though covered with the pelt of some strange animal. High in the web of bare branches, the clumps of mistletoe showed as filigree nests for some race of fairy birds.

Gracious country this, for all the desolate whiteness; it lay in great rolling slopes with drifts of purplish elms in the folds, and on the levels winding steel-dark streams along whose banks the upward-springing willows burned an ardent rust colour. And as the car rocked and bounded along and the wind screen first starred in one place, then in another, then fell out altogether, one got a better and better view of it all.

What a wonderful people the French are for agriculture. . . . Hardly a man did I see all the days I motored about and about, but I saw mile after mile of cultivated land, the sombrely-clad women or boys guiding the slow ploughs, the rough-coated horses pulling patiently—white horses that looked pale against the bare earth, but a dark yellow when the snow came to show up the tarnishing that the service of man brings upon beasts. Several times I saw English soldiers ploughing, and rejoiced.

We came into the town that was our bourn in the grey of the evening, passed the grey glimmer of the river between its grey stone quays, passed the grey miracle of the cathedral, and then, in the rapidly deepening dusk, turned in through great wrought iron gates into a grey courtyard.

It may have been gathered that, much as I admire both their practical perfection and their spiritual significance, I am no lover of camps, which seem to me among all things man-created upon God's earth about the most depressing. I had lived and moved and had my being in camps it seemed to me for countless ages, the edges of my soul were frayed with camps. From the moment of walking into the old house at R—— a wonderful sense of rest that brooded over the place enveloped me. The thing had an atmosphere, impossible to exaggerate, though very difficult to convey, but I shall never forget the miracle that house was to me.

It was a Hostel for the Relations of Wounded,

and there are in France at present some half-dozen of these houses, supported by the Joint War Committee of the Red Cross and the Order of St. John, and staffed by V.A.D.'s. At all of them the relations of badly wounded are lodged and fed free of charge, while cars meet them and also convey them to and from the hospital. This much I knew as plain facts, what I had not been prepared for was the breath of exquisite pleasure that emanated from this house.

The house was originally a butter market, and the entrance room, set about with little tables where the relations have their meals, has one side entirely of glass; the lounge beyond, which is for the staff, is glass-roofed, while that opening on the right hand of the dining-place, the lounge for the relations, has long windows all down the side; so it will be seen that light and air are abundant on the ground floor of the Hostel in spite of the fact that it looks on to a courtyard.

From the relations' lounge, with its slim vermilion pillars ringed about with seats like those round tree-trunks, there goes up a curving staircase of red tiles, with a carved baluster of oak greyish with age, a griffon sitting upright upon the newel. Up this staircase I was taken to my room, and there the completion of peace came upon me.

One could see at a glance it would be quiet, beautifully quiet. Its window gave on to the sloping grey flanks of pointed roofs and showed a filigree spire pricking the pale bubble of the wintry sky, its walls were panelled from floor to ceiling, its hangings were of white and vermilion, its floor dark and polished, and on the wide stone hearth burned a wood fire. And, to crown all, after tiny huts, it was so big a room that the corners were filled with gracious shadow; and the firelight flickered up and down on the panelling and glimmered in the polished floor and set the shadows quivering. I lay back in a vermilion-painted chair and felt steeped in the bath of restfulness that the place was.

The whole house was very perfectly "got-up," the maximum of effect having been attained with the minimum of expense, though not of labour; it all having been achieved under the direction of a former superintendent with a genius for decoration, who is now V.A.D. Area Commandant and still lives at the Hostel. The evening I arrived there, she and the staff were busy stenciling a buff bedspread with blue galleons in full sail, varied by gulls. Everything is exceedingly simple, there is no fussy detail, nothing to catch dirt. The walls are all panelled, and painted either ivory or dark brown; the furniture is of wicker and plain wood, painted in gay colours—rich blues and vermilion; the tablecloths are of red or blue checks. In the spacious bedrooms are simple colour schemes—in one there are thick, straight curtains of flaming orange, in another of a deep blue, in another of red and white checked material. The floors are of polished wood or red tiles strewn with rugs; vivid-coloured cushions lie in the easy chairs; and set about in earthen jars are great branches of mimosa and lilac from the South, boughs of pussy-willow, the tender velvety grey ovals blossoming into fragile yellow dust; all along the sills are indoor window-boxes filled with hyacinths of pink and white and a cold faint blue.

. On the walls the only decoration is that of posters, and these create an extraordinary effect as of a series of windows, opening upon different climes and strange worlds, windows set in ivory walls. Here is an old Norman castle, grey against a sky of luminous yellow, there a stream in Brittany which you can almost hear brawling past the plane-trees with their freckled trunks, while beyond it, through another window, you see a pergola of roses whose deep red has turned wine-coloured under the moonlight, and beyond that again, the white cliffs of England go down into a peacock sea. And, in the Red Cross dining-room, a poilu, his mouth open on a yell of encouragement, 'charges with uplifted hands, looking over his shoulder at you with bright daring eyes, and you do not need the inscription underneath of *"On les aura!"* to guess what spirit urges him.

This, then, is the setting for one of the most

merciful of the works of the Red Cross. That it is appreciated is shown by the fact that at Christmas, at this house, with its staff of Superintendent, cook, parlourmaid, housemaid and "tweeny," with one chauffeuse, there were forty relations of wounded staying. The average number of people for whom Army and Red Cross rations are drawn three times a week is twenty-five, but for these rations as for fifteen are drawn, as the food supply is too generously proportioned for a household consisting so largely of women. But it will be seen that with a constantly fluctuating population the task of housekeeping is no easy one, though it is tackled by the voluntary staff with gaiety and courage.

They have troubles of their own, too, the members of that staff, and in the big kitchen, where among the dishes on the table a pink hyacinth bloomed, the fair-haired cook I saw so busily working was back from a leave in England that was to have been her marriage-leave, had not her fiancé been killed the day before he was to join her. Now she is amongst her pots and pans again and smiling still, as I can testify. The "tweeny," who also describes herself as a boot-boy, is a young war-widow. Things like these are almost beyond the admiration of mortals less severely tested.

The material difficulties are not the worst in a hostel of this kind, which in its very nature presupposes grief. The relations, of course, are of all kinds, after every pattern of humanity, and each makes his or her emotional demand, if not in active appeal to sympathy, yet in the strain that it entails on the sensitively organised to see others in sorrow—and unless you are sensitive you are no good for work such as this. This hostel is blessed in its Superintendent, an American V.A.D. worker of a personality so *simpatica*—there is no adequate English for what I mean—that you are aware of it at first meeting with her; and she is a woman of the world, which is not always the case with women workers, however excellent.

Shortly before I came to the Hostel a very young wife arrived to see her husband, who lay desperately ill in one of the hospitals. When he died she became as a thing distraught and could not be left, and the Superintendent even had to have her to sleep in her room with her all the time she was there. Others, again, are aloof in their sorrow, though it is none the less tragic for that. The first question on the lips of the Staff when the chauffeuse comes back from taking the relatives to the hospital is, "Was it good news?"

It was good news for the couple who arrived on the same evening that I did, the mother and father of a young officer who was very badly injured. I saw them next morning in the lounge, sitting quietly on either sire of the centre-stove, a business man and his wife, as neat, he in his serge suit, she in her satin blouse and carefully folded lace and smooth grey hair, as if they had not been travelling for a day and a night on end, racked by anxiety, though you could see the deep lines that the strain had left. He looked at me with those patient eyes of the elderly which hold the same unconscious pathos as those of animals, and talked in a low quiet voice, and it seemed almost an impertinence of a total stranger to assure these gentle, dignified people of her gladness that their only son was safe, yet how glad one is that any one of these brief contacts in passing should be of happiness! It is so impossible not to weep with them that weep that it is a keen joy to be able to rejoice with them that do rejoice.

"It's so free here . . ." he told me, "that's what the wife and I like so. No rules and regulations, you can do just what you like as though you were in your own home . . . no feeling that as you don't pay you've got to do what you're told." And there was expressed the spirit of the Hostel as I discovered it.

There are no rules, and it is always impressed upon the Superintendents that the relations are not obliged to go there, that they do so because they choose to, and must be treated as honoured guests. In the dining-room there are little tables as at an hotel, so that the different parties can keep to themselves if they prefer it; there are no times for going out or coming in, no times for "lights out," no need to have a meal in if the visitor mentions he is going out for it. The relations who stay at these hostels are guests in every sense of the word, and there is not one trace of red tape or the faintest feeling of obligation about the whole thing.

And that must have been what I had felt in the very air of the place when I arrived, what stole with so precious a balm over me who had been in camp after camp, institution after institution. This place, with its quiet walls and its grey shutters wing-wide upon its grey walls, was not only beautiful and rich with that richness only age can give, it was instinct as well with freedom and with peace.

# CHAPTER XIII

## GENERAL SERVANTS AND A GENERAL QUESTION

I HAVE left till the last what to some people
will be the dullest and what is certainly the least
spectacular of all the work done by the women
in France, but what is to me perhaps the most
wonderful and admirable of all. I mean that of
the Domestic Staffs.

For there is something thrilling about driving
wounded, something eternally picturesque about
nursing them, but there is no glamour about being
a general servant. . . . A general servant, year
in, year out, and with no wages at that, for I talk
of the voluntary staffs, girls of gentle birth and
breeding who deliberately undertake to wash
dishes and clean floors and empty slops day after
day. I think heroism can no higher go, and I
am not trying to be funny; I mean it.

All the voluntary camps I had seen, all the
hostels, the rest stations, and many hospitals, are
staffed by voluntary domestic help; and the girls
they wait upon, the drivers and secretaries and
such like, are eager in recognition of them. But
that seems to me about all the recognition they do

get; they get no "snappy pars," no photographs in the picture papers, no songs are sung of them, no reward is theirs in the shape of medal or ribbon, nothing but the sense of a dish properly cleaned or rugs duly swept under. I consider that there ought to be a special medal for girls who have slaved as general servants during the war, without a thrill of romance to support them; a "Skivvy's Ribbon" as one of them laughingly suggested to me when I propounded the idea.

Take, for example, the Headquarters of the British Red Cross, at the Hotel Christol at Boulogne, to which I returned on my homeward way, as I had come to it on landing. The staff, counting the Commissioner and officials, the clerks, typists, secretaries, and Post Office girls, amount to about a hundred and forty-five people, and the house staff number seventeen and are all V.A.D.'s. The Hotel Christol is also the headquarters for all Red Cross people going on leave or arriving therefrom via Boulogne, and all have to report there; nearly all want a meal, many want a bed.

The men-workers and many of the women, such as V.A.D. Commandants, etc., live out in billets in the town, but the manageress and her assistant, the Post Office Commandant, the girl driver of the mail-car with her orderly (these two girls drive about sixty miles daily with the mails), the girls of the telephone exchange and the rest of the Post Office girls, all "live in," and in addition

to the casual Red Cross workers who may appeal
for a bed any time there are the relations of
wounded who have been put up there whenever
possible, though now a hostel is being opened in
Boulogne for the purpose. All the people working
in the house and all Red Cross workers arriving
by boat are entitled to take their meals at the
Christol, as are all Red Cross workers in Boulogne, both officers and privates, and the average
number of meals served is 2,500 a week. Four
or five girls act as waitresses in the dining-room,
and three are always in the pantry, which must
never be left for a moment during the day; so it
will be seen that the headquarters of the Red
Cross is a sort of hotel, except that nobody pays.

There are French servants to do the roughest
work, but the girls have plenty to do without that.
The house staff begin work at seven in the morning; at seven-thirty in the evening they start to
turn out the forty-two offices, which they sweep
and dust every day. They wash all the tea-things
(not the dinner-things), and clean all the silver
and glass, they make the beds and do all the waiting. A pretty good list of occupations, is it not,
carried out on such a huge scale?

The girls are well looked after, for it must not
be forgotten that some of them are not more than
eighteen, and their parents in England have a
right to demand that these children should be at
once guarded and cheered. No Red Cross girl

is allowed out after half-past nine in a restaurant, and none is ever allowed to dine out unaccompanied by another girl. But when a friend of a girl passes through Boulogne, then it is permitted that she and another girl may go and dine with the officer in question, always provided they are back by nine-thirty. For superiors are merciful and human creatures these days, and there is always the thought that the girl may never see that friend again. And Heaven—and the superior—knows that these girls need and deserve a little relaxation and enjoyment.

And would you not think that to girls who work as these do and behave so well would at least be given the understanding and respect of all of us who do so much less? Yet how often one hears careless remarks of censure or—worse—of belittlement. That to other nations our ways may need explaining is understandable, but we should indeed be ashamed that any amongst ourselves fail in comprehension.

What do the French think of our women? That is a question that inevitably arises in the mind of anyone who knows the differences in French and English education. Let me show the thing as I think it is, by means of a metaphor.

It is universally conceded that marriage is a more difficult proposition than friendship, that it is more a test of affection to live under one roof and share the daily commonplaces of life than it is to meet occasionally when one can make a feast of the meeting. Yet this is not to say that marriage is the less admirable state, but only to allow that it is one requiring greater sacrifices, greater tact, and—greater affection. Therefore, when it is admitted that the presence in France for nearly four years of English soldiers, English civilians on war-work, and the consequent erection of whole temporary townships for their accommodation, is a greater test—if you will a greater strain—for the Entente than if intercourse had been limited to an occasional interchange of a handful of people, one is not saying anything derogatory either to French hosts or English guests, but merely frankly conceding that more depth of affection and understanding is necessary than would otherwise have been the case. To superficial relationships, superficial knowledge, but to the big partnerships of life, complete understanding. And, if that is never quite possible in this world, at least let the corner where knowledge cannot come be filled by tolerance.

England is no longer on terms of mere friendly intercourse with France; the bond is deeper, more indissoluble. . . . And as in marriage the closest bond of all is the birth of children, so in this pact of nations the greatest bond is the loss of children—lost for the same cause upon the same soil. . . .

With a bond as deep as this—a bond always

acknowledged and given its meed of recognition by the most thoughtful brains and sensitive hearts —yet, as in marriage, there are bound to be minor irritations, points, not of meeting, but of conflict. Trifles, indeed, these points, compared with the magnitude of the bond which unites, but nevertheless trifles which would be better adjusted than ignored.

In the first place, we must recognise that though the things which unite us, our common ideals, our common needs, are far stronger than any difference in our modes of thought, yet those differences exist, and that, in marriage, it is often said that it is the little things which count. . . . Heaven forbid that we should so lose sense of proportion as to say it when the matter in hand is the marriage of nations, but nevertheless it is well not entirely to forget it. . . . And, of all the differences in customs between us, there is probably none more marked than in our way of treating what is known—loosely and with considerable banality—as the "sex-problem." This is not the place to discuss those differences, though, as one who has known and loved France all her life, I may mention that, personally, I see much to admire in the French system and could wish that we emulated it, but that is neither here nor there at the moment.

France has probably evolved for the happiness and welfare of her womenkind the sort of life

which suits best with their temperament and circumstances. Women, like water, find their own
level, and no one who knows France, and knows
the devotion, the business capacity, and the good
works of her women, imagines them to be the butterfly creatures that English fancy used to paint
them twenty or thirty years ago. As a matter of
fact, the present writer had occasion, two winters
ago, to make a close study of the varied scope of
women's work in France—the hospitals for training of *femmes du monde,* the schools like Le
Foyer, for the training of young girls of the upper
classes to help their poorer sisters, etc., etc., all
works carried on unostentatiously long before the
war broke upon us and proved their usefulness.
The "butterfly" Frenchwoman underwent, before
the war, a far more serious social training than
did the happy-go-lucky English girl, and was better equipped in consequence, with a knowledge of
economic conditions, than the untrained English-
woman could be.

But we too have our quality, and I rather think
it is to be found in the greater freedom which we
are allowed. We were not so well trained, but
freedom stepped into the place of custom, and
gave the necessary attitude of mind—that unprejudiced, untrammelled attitude which is essential
to the quick grasping of a fresh *métier.* That is
where our method—or, if you prefer it, our lack
of method—helped us, even as their training

helped the French. And the French, with their extraordinary facility of vision, do, I think, understand that we have simply pushed our freedom to its logical and legitimate outcome, that we could not be expected, after being accustomed, for many years past, to be on terms of simple easy friendship with men as with our own sex, above all, after working side by side with them since this war began, we could not be expected to say that we could not work with them in France, though we could in England, or that perhaps this girl would, and that girl couldn't. . . .

We naturally proceeded to act *en masse* as we had acted individually, to do on a large scale what had been done on a small, to manipulate great bodies of women where before a few friends had worked together. In every large body of persons there are bound to be one or two individuals who fail to come up to the required standard, but that does not alter the principle that what can safely be done in small quantities can safely be done in large, provided the conditions are altered to scale.

And that is what we are doing, and what our Government is helping us to do; that is what our Women's Army and our voluntary workers in France are—the expression, on a large scale, of what bands of women have been doing so successfully on a small scale since the beginning of the war—helping, and even replacing the men.

And just as, with our peculiar training and mode
of thought, it is possible for the average English-
woman to eliminate sex as a factor in the scheme
of things, so it is possible to eliminate it in greater
masses.   In other words, it is perfectly possible,
to men and girls brought up with the English
method of free friendly intercourse, to work side
by side, to meet, to walk together, and to remain
—merely friends.   Whether that is a good thing
or not is another point altogether, as it is whether
it makes for charm in a woman. . . . Certainly
no woman in this world competes with a Frenchwoman for charm.   It is as recognised as an Eng-
lishwoman's complexion—and considerably more
lasting!

Probably it is only ourselves and the Ameri-
cans among the races of the world who could have
instituted such an experiment as that of our Wom-
en's Army, but there is among the nations one
which is supreme in "flair," in sympathy, and a
certain ability to comprehend intellectually what
it might not understand emotionally, and that nation is France.

I am confident that it will never have to be said
that when Englishwomen sacrificed so much—and
to a Frenchwoman one does not need to point
out what a sacrifice it is when a woman risks youth
and looks in hard unceasing work—that French-
women failed to understand them or to attribute
motives to them other than those that have ani-

mated themselves in their own labours throughout the war.

That it must sometimes look odd to them one knows so well; how can it be otherwise? They see the girls, khaki-clad, out walking without "Tommies," hear the sounds of music and dancing coming from the recreation huts, where the girls are allowed to invite the men, and *vice versa*. Yet, if you investigate, you will find out that they are of an extraordinary simplicity, these girls and men, in their intercourse, in their earnest dancing, taught them by instructors from our Young Men's Christian Association, inspired by nothing more heady than lemonade, and chaperoned by the women-officers, who have attained a mixture of authority and motherly supervision over every individual girl that reminds me of nothing so much as the care, born of a sort of divine cunning, of a very dear and clever Mother Superior at a convent I once stayed at in France. For the interesting point for both the French and ourselves to note is that in the treatment of our Women's Army in France we have taken a leaf out of their book. We look after the girls with something of that love and care which surrounds a girl in France.

For many of the Women's Army are working girls, who have never been guarded in their lives, whose parents had probably, after the lower-class English way, very little influence with them, and who, though good, honest, rough girls, were free to roam the streets of their native towns with their friends every evening once their work was over. Now, for what is for many of them the first time in their lives, they are being watched and guarded in a manner that is more French than English, and which I find admirable. As for their walks, their friendships with men, the personal observation of the acute French will show them that it is merely our Anglo-Saxon way, and the official statistics will prove to any doubters how well both the girls and the men can be trusted to behave themselves. We are a cold nation if you like, but there 'it is—it has its excellences, if not its charms.

So much for fundamental differences, which, when intelligence and sympathy go out to meet them, become merely points on which temperaments agree to differ amicably, each giving its meed of admiration to the other. And for minor matters, little things of different customs only, that nevertheless, occasionally, in the strain of this war, ruffle even friends, I would say something like this, which is in the hearts of us all . . .

France—dear lovely France, to so many of us adored for many years, who has stood to us for the romance of the world, we know that in many things our ways are not your ways and never will be, nor would we wish it otherwise. To each nation her distinctiveness, or she loses her soul.

But, when those ways of ours seem to you most
alien, say to yourself: "This is only England's
differing way of doing what we are doing, of fighting for what we are fighting for—the saving of
the right to individualism, the right to be different. . . ." To gain that we are all having to become alike, just as to win freedom we are having
for a time to give it up, and the great thing to remember is that this terrible coherent community
life is being borne with only that eventually we
may all be free men once more. Let us, for all
time, differ in our own ways, rather than agree
in the German! But also let us, while differing,
understand.

# CHAPTER XIV

## NOTES AND QUERIES

ON my last evening I sat and thought about the girls I had seen and known, in greater and less degrees, in passing. And I saw them, not as unthinking "sporting" young things, who were having a great adventure, but as girls who were steadily sticking to their jobs, often without enjoyment save that of knowledge of good work well done. And I thought of those prophets who gloomily foretell that the women will never want to drop into the background again—forgetful of the fact that where a woman is is never a background to herself. I smiled as I thought of the eagerness with which these hard workers in mud and snow and heat will start buying pretty clothes again and going out to parties . . . and I was very thankful to know how unchangedly woman they had all remained, in spite of the fact that they had had the strength to lay the privileges and the fun of being a woman aside for a time.

I remembered what the D. of T. had said to me when we discussed the question of how the girls would settle down when it was all over, and how he had thought that even if they did not marry all would be well, because they would have had their adventure. . . . I remembered too how that had seemed to me the correct answer at the time. Then later, when that awful web of depression caught me, and the horror of the school-girl conditions of life and all the apparent "brightness" had choked me, I had all the more thought it true, but marvelled; later still, when I caught glimpses of that wonderful spirit and that deep sophistication which had so cheered me, I reversed the whole judgment and thought there was nothing in it.

Now, thinking it all over, it seemed to me that somewhere midway lay Truth. These girls have had, in a certain sense, their adventure, but when it is all over, they will have a reaction from it, and I believe that reaction will be pleasant to them, that it will be the reaction, and not the memory of adventure, which will content them. It is certain that to anyone who has worked as these girls work a considerable period of doing nothing in particular will be very acceptable. They will all have to become themselves again, which will be interesting. . . .

Dear, wonderful girls . . . you who wash dishes and scrub and sweep, you girls of the Women's Army who replace men and who do it so thoroughly, you drivers who are out in all weathers, night and day, sometimes for a week or more on end, who face hardships such as were faced in those three weeks at T—— when there were no fires and no water, how glad I am to have met you. . . . So I sat and thought, and then I picked up a copy of *The Times* which had just come over. And in the "Personal" column this caught my eye:

"Lady wants war-work, preferably motor-driving, from three to five p.m."

And I saw that it was not only those far removed from the war who misunderstood both what it demands and that which has arisen to meet those demands.

Do we not nearly all fail to realise the magnitude and import of what is being done by these unspectacular workers behind the lines, who are yet part of war itself, and daily and nightly strengthen the hands of the fighters? Some of us in England realise as little as you in far-off countries, and yet it should be our business to know, because the least we can do is to understand so that we, in our much less fine way, can help them a little, one tithe of the amount they help our fighting men.

Not because of any desire of theirs for praise is it necessary—I never saw a healthier disregard, amounting to a kindly contempt, for what those at home think or don't think, than among the women working in France—but because it is only by knowing that we can respond generously enough to the needs of their work, and only by understanding that we can save our own souls from that fat and contented ignorance which induces a sleep uncommonly like death.

Nor, as long as we listen to the girls themselves, are we in any danger of thinking too much of them or of their work.  Not a woman I met, English or American, working in France, but said something like this, and meant it: "What, after all, is anything we can do, except inasmuch as it may help the men a little?  How could we bear to do nothing when the men are doing the most wonderful thing that has ever been done in the world?"

**THE END**

Lightning Source UK Ltd.
Milton Keynes UK
UKHW020705080722
405572UK00006B/468